Sherlock Holmes and

The Last Victim of

Jack The Ripper

By

Petr Macek

Paperback ISBN 978-1-80424-537-8
ePub ISBN 978-1-80424-538-5
PDF ISBN 978-1-80424-539-2

Published by MX Publishing
335 Princess Park Manor, Royal Drive,
London, N11 3GX
www.mxpublishing.co.uk

Cover design by Awan
Translated from Czech edition by Klara Pruchova
Edited by Jamie Marshall

Contents

DEATH BEFORE COCKCROW

Morgan Davis hanged herself on the night of the 2nd of February in the lavatories of the St. Ignatius Catholic School. The incident could have posed grave problems for the institute, which aimed to educate young ladies from the upper classes and prepare them for wedlock, as the poor girl had left a farewell letter, in which she cited torment and persecution by her fellow schoolmates and dormitory lodgers as the reason for her voluntary departure from this world. The school had the reputation of being one of the most rigorous yet prestigious facilities of its kind in England, and its headmaster was among the many acquaintances of Mycroft Holmes, brother of my dear friend, Sherlock Holmes, whose cases I regularly put on record. By way of Mycroft's influence, therefore, the detective and I found ourselves on the scene shortly after the body was discovered.

Yet I have hesitated for quite some time in putting this adventure to paper, for the mere recollection of this deplorable crime, which ended in the death of a thirteen-year-old girl, makes my soul uneasy. Nevertheless, as the topic is of grave social significance, I feel it is right for my readers to finally learn the truth. For what ran in the press at the time was but a mild derivative of the facts.

The headmaster of the school, the much-respected Mr. Oliver Schaffer, was awaiting us impatiently. His appearance was so distressed that, had his tousled hair not already been streaked with silver, doubtless it would have gone quite white after the events of that morning.

He led us through the icy halls of the boarding school, his scarlet gown fluttering a few steps ahead of us, and before every turn he peeked cautiously around the corner to ascertain that the way was clear. "At present, only my deputy, the maid who found her, and of course the doctor who was called in, know anything of the tragedy. I didn't want to raise a fuss before the matter was duly investigated. Miss Davis hails from a very high-ranking family, and her older brother is soon to take over her father's peerage in the House of Lords," he whispered.

Lessons had already begun, and the long corridors of the school were, fortunately for the headmaster, entirely devoid of people. Only our own hurried steps resounded on the polished stone floor, which reflected the first cool rays of the morning sun falling through the tall windows.

"Children can be very cruel," I sighed. "Often unconsciously and without malintent. In their immature minds, they are unable to estimate the boundaries of what is fun and humorous to them, yet degrading to the point of self-destructive psychic problems for others."

"Indeed. Nonetheless, they often show an inclination towards deliberate sadism and the desire to injure even at a very young age," countered the detective. "As always, my dear Watson, you strive to see the world through the prism of your natural kindness. I, however, am a realist. I know that evil is present in creatures of every age."

Schaffer listened to our dialogue with growing dismay.

"I've never encountered such a thing in all my career," he retorted. "Our pupils are raised to lead respectable lives and love their kin. Why, their very pedigree guarantees high moral standards. What you speak of has no place at our school."

Holmes did not raise his voice, in respect of the headmaster's wish to deal with the affair without needless fuss, but still his words stung like whip. "Blood does not run blue in some and red in others," he said searingly. "Nor does pedigree guarantee kindness. I could name more than a few well-situated noblemen whom I've convicted of heinous crimes."

If there was one thing Holmes despised, it was bigotry, signs of which he had noticed in the headmaster's speech.

"If, indeed, somebody has driven Miss Davis to her final act, I intend to investigate the matter, identify the culprit and hold them accountable. And I should point out beforehand that their age or social status are of no significance whatsoever to me," he added curtly.

By then we had reached the scene of the incident.

The door to the lavatory was locked, with a sign affixed at eye level that read "Out of order." To make sure, Schaffer's deputy, a rather younger professor with a keen eye, kept watch. Quite unlike the dishevelled and flustered headmaster, we were met by a man with a ramrod spine, carefully coiffed and attired in a well-fitted suit of clothing with polished shoes.

"John Riesling," he introduced himself, shaking our hands in turn. He had a firm, dry grasp, unlike his superior, whose handshake had been nervous with rather clammy palms. "Nobody has entered except for the doctor."

The detective absorbed this information. His eyebrows drew together over his aquiline nose like two oncoming trains, and with a deep intake of breath, preparing his mind for what he was about to see, he had the door unlocked and grasped the handle. I entered immediately behind him, followed by the two schoolteachers.

I will refrain from depicting the sombre scene that opened before us. Excessive descriptiveness has no part in the case. I myself am not of an overly sensitive disposition, but I must consider the possibility that Morgan's relations might read this text, and they would doubtless be aggrieved even after so many years.

The lavatories on this floor consisted of ten stalls fitted with locks, in two rows of five facing each other. The stall doors did not reach from floor to ceiling, as is usually the case, but instead ended some eight inches above the threshold. A space of at least a yard separated the upper doorframe from the ceiling, which was criss-crossed by the gas pipelines that snaked through the entire building.

At the end of the elongated room, a skylight looked out onto the courtyard. The tiled wall nearer the entrance was festooned with porcelain washbasins and towel racks. Above them hung dull mirrors, and the cheerless scene was underscored by the flickering glow of an electric light.

A tall, bony man wearing a pince-nez stood near the skylight, staring blankly into space with reddish eyes. He had loosened his stiff shirt collar and his bowler hat was pushed so far back on his head that I was surprised it hadn't fallen off. He kneaded a cigarette butt between this thumb and index finger, pulling on it absentmindedly without realising it had gone out.

"Professor Haggins, the school physician," piped up Schaffer behind us.

The doctor blinked and fixed us with a pitying gaze.

"There was nothing I could do. She was dead long before I arrived," he said flatly in lieu of a greeting.

He had already freed Morgan's body from the noose and had laid it on the floor. Her eyes were closed and in her pure white nightgown, she looked quite like a sleeping angel, except for the hideous red line from the rope that had snaked around her neck and cut into her soft child's skin. The door of the penultimate stall stood wide open, and a pair of discarded slippers lay nearby. The other end of the cut rope was still hanging from one of the gas pipes beneath the ceiling.

It was all I could do to control my senses, as a chill passed down my spine.

"Have you moved anything?" Holmes asked Haggins.

"I had to take her down. I couldn't…" the physician's voice stuttered, but he regained himself and continued. "I couldn't just leave her hanging there like that."

"Quite so," the detective reassured him.

"She was discovered here around five o'clock this morning, before dawn, during cleaning," Riesling chimed in. "The other girls were still asleep in the dormitory, so nobody had noticed she was missing. She must have crept in during the night."

"Judging by the stiffness of the body, I would guess that she died between one and two o'clock after midnight," Haggins added. "Mind, I am not a medical examiner like you…"

His estimate precisely matched mine, at least based on my general examination of the corpse. Nor was there any doubt as to the cause of death, so I merely confirmed what had been said. Neither of us intended to question the school physician's expertise, but my friend did prefer to rely on my expert opinion, albeit he often managed on his own.

"Were there any signs on the body of the grievances she claimed to have suffered? Torn hair, bumps, bruises, scratches or scrapes?" inquired Holmes.

"I noticed nothing of the kind, either today or ever," the doctor confided.

We had no reason to doubt his words, as he appeared to be a thorough and caring individual.

"Where is the suicide note? May I see it?" Holmes turned to the headmaster.

"In my office."

"Any tampering with the evidence makes my job very difficult," the detective frowned once again.

"My mistake," admitted the deputy headmaster. "I acted on impulse, and when the doctor and I found the letter, I took it to Mr. Schaffer. I do apologise."

Holmes sighed. "Very well. I shall examine it later," he said, heading towards the stall where Morgan had chosen to kill herself. "Was Miss Davis talented in sports?"

"Like any normal thirteen-year-old girl," Riesling shrugged. "I shouldn't think she was in any way exceptional, although she did enjoy ball games. Why do you ask?"

"She performed quite the athletic feat before her death," the detective mused, gazing up at the ceiling. "By all accounts, she must have climbed onto the doorframe, pulled the rope up and attached it to the pipe. I can see even from here that she opted for a nautical knot. Are the girls at your school commonly taught those? Perhaps during embroidery lessons?"

"I don't know what you are implying," Schaffer frowned, displeased with the tone in which Holmes had started speaking to him. Likely, he had imagined the investigation would take a rather different turn when he had asked Mycroft for help.

"Oh, I'm merely thinking aloud," Holmes reassured him.

His undisguised scepticism seemed to have affected me, too.

"Nor do I see any chair or stool that she may have jumped from," I remarked.

"Most likely she stood on the toilet bowl, slipped the noose around her neck and threw herself off," suggested Haggins, closing his medical bag. "A chair could make noise while falling over and wake somebody up."

"Certainly, quite possible," my friend conceded. "Miss Davis was remarkably considerate towards her alleged tormentors, despite having decided to end her life," he said, unable to resist yet another snide comment.

It was obvious to me that something was amiss.

But Holmes appeared to have finished here. "Gentlemen, I do believe it is high time we allowed Miss Davis to rest in peace," he commanded. "Dr. Haggins, would you ensure that her body is taken to the morgue quietly and out of sight of inquisitive eyes? The child deserves some respect."

"Of course."

"Excellent. I would have one more favour to ask. I will need the rope she used for further analysis. Both ends," Holmes pointed to the noose and to the other segment below the ceiling. "Could you please arrange this?"

"Certainly," the doctor nodded again.

"Thank you," the detective said, departing. "The rest of us shall carry on."

Schaffer and Riesling returned down the corridor with us, waiting to see what Holmes would produce next.

Naturally, the chief item on his mind was the farewell letter. We proceeded to the headmaster's office, which in no way reflected the austerity of the furnishings in the girls' school and boarding house. Upon seating ourselves on a comfortable leather divan and receiving a cup of coffee (which

I greatly appreciated given the busy morning), Schaffer removed the epistle from his desk drawer.

Holmes perused it impatiently, running his fingertips over its surface, and then turned it over several times, examining it minutely.

"I see you have some doubts. The writing is unquestionably Morgan's. I know it well. She is in my natural sciences class, and I correct her work every day," Riesling confirmed the authenticity of the letter.

"It would seem I've met my match in terms of reading body language," the detective replied. "But I suspect you haven't a clue as to what I am actually thinking."

By now, even I was taken aback by the antagonism with which Holmes treated the school's representatives.

"Has the young lady made any similar attempts in the past?" I inquired.

"No, not in the two years she has spent at our establishment," Schaffer replied, choosing to ignore Holmes. "But one incident allegedly did occur before she joined us. It was shortly after her mother's death. Unfortunately, I am unfamiliar with the details."

My friend tsked in annoyance and handed me the letter, which seemed to have entirely lost his interest. It was covered in small, neat handwriting, pressed to the upper edge of the page. The words, phrasing and articulation indicated a writer of profound sensibility and rich imagination. She complained that nobody understood or comprehended her, and that she was being mistreated by an unnamed person.

Indeed, she found life pointless as a whole.

"I would now like to see the bedroom where the young lady slept. Preferably before some diligent busybody decides to clean it," Holmes asked the two teachers while I devoured the letter. "Then I would like to meet her classmates and all your students, who might have any knowledge of harassment on the school premises. I must question all of them thoroughly, ideally before noon."

The headmaster's face flushed with suppressed indignation. "I am not certain their parents would consent to such actions," he sputtered, the steam building up in him. "After all, they are but children."

Holmes gazed down at him in a condescending manner. "My esteemed headmaster," he said, "it grieves me that in your arrogance you fail to see that I am acting in your own best interest, first and foremost. Is that not why I was summoned? Believe me, it is essential."

The strength and authority of Sherlock Holmes's personality impressed the fuming head of the institution, as it had so many others before and afterwards.

"Very well, very well," he muttered resignedly, dropping his head into his hands. "I shall not hinder you in anything."

"Have you already informed Miss Davis's family of her passing?"

"Not yet. I intended to wait until after your visit."

"Then do hold it off another few hours. They deserve to receive complete information, not mere speculations. I shall inform you of the results of my investigation as soon as I can."

We left the exasperated headmaster to his woes and had his deputy guide us to the school's boarding house, where the students were lodged. Here, Riesling introduced the house mistress, Mrs. MacDonnell.

The austere, elderly lady had learned of Morgan Davis's fate only moments ago, and had not yet managed to overcome the shock. She was wringing a lace handkerchief in her hands.

"Yes indeed, relationships in girls' groups can sometimes be strained, but I didn't notice anything that could have induced Morgan to take her own life," she sobbed. "Just childish pranks, minor squabbles and petty banter."

She led us through a large, well-lit room that served as a bedroom for eight girls. None of the young ladies lodging at the boarding house had private quarters – all the rooms were shared by six to ten girls. The bedrooms were sparsely furnished, to the point of being almost spartan. Each girl had nothing but a bed, a nightstand, a small cabinet for personal items and a wardrobe.

Given the exorbitant tuition fees and the fact that the institution was intended for girls from affluent families, I found their stark living conditions rather striking.

"It is precisely for this reason that our school is so highly regarded by their families," Mrs. MacDonnell explained somewhat testily, dabbing at her puffy eyes. "We guide the girls towards the utmost modesty, strive to detach them from material extravagance and encourage their lasting spiritual blossoming."

"What can you tell us about Morgan's character," the detective inquired.

"She joined us about a year after her father, Lord Davis, was widowed. He himself is gravely ill and Morgan's brother, the young master, Stewart Davis, is not among the most responsible guardians. The young lady lacked proper upbringing and education. She was ten when she arrived at our school. For the first few months, she was rather rebellious and stubborn, but this changed, and our relationship improved. She was a gentle, sensitive girl with superb academic results."

"Did she fit into the collective?"

"I can't say that she had a bosom friend among the other girls, but I am not aware of an explicit rival either."

"In her farewell letter, Morgan wrote of mistreatment," I recalled.

"I strongly deny any suggestion that it came from me or any other of the teaching staff," Mrs. MacDonnell declared adamantly. "Nor is corporal punishment used here."

The detective browsed the bedroom, minutely examining every detail. "Are the girls under constant supervision, or might something have happened between them at some unguarded moment when they were alone? I find it hard to believe she made it up."

"This is not Newgate, Mr. Holmes," the house mistress retorted, with reference to the infamous London prison. "The girls have precisely as much privacy as they require. During lessons they are with their teachers, and then the governesses take over. We are responsible for them, so they are naturally under standard supervision. I repeat, I have no knowledge of any mistreatment."

Holmes paused near the only unmade bed in the room.

"We left everything just as Morgan had left it, like you requested," said Mrs. MacDonnell.

Holmes nodded in satisfaction and looked through all the compartments and drawers in the cabinet, as well as the closet. He found nothing to puzzle or disquiet him.

On the nightstand was a stoneware jug and empty glass. The detective peered into the jug and inhaled the sweetish odour of the dark liquid at the bottom.

"Grape juice," he remarked.

"Our wards only drink clean water," said the house mistress in surprise. "We do not serve them sweet beverages or wine."

"How odd," pondered Holmes. "But not criminal. She may have procured it in the kitchen. Perhaps Morgan was feeling peckish before bedtime?"

"I wouldn't be surprised. Morgan had rather a sweet tooth," she agreed.

When my friend had finished examining the bedroom, he asked Riesling and MacDonnell to arrange a meeting with the other wards. They were questioned in the faculty room, in the presence of the teachers but without any duress put on the children by the adults. Holmes was gentle and considerate, but spared them not at all. His questions were probing, straightforward and he made it clear to the girls that it was a very grave matter indeed.

Yet try as he might, he discovered nothing more about any harassment in the group.

"I'm sorry you've travelled so far for nothing," sighed Riesling after the last girls had left. "I can think of nothing that could shed more light on the circumstances of Morgan's death."

"I don't find my work to have been futile. Do you?" exclaimed Holmes is surprise.

"I did not wish to offend you," the deputy headmaster replied, alarmed.

"I am not offended. I've long since become used to seeing what others are either blind to, do not wish to see, or are incapable of connecting."

The last stop on our tour of the school was the kitchen, situated in the nether regions of the building.

The place was a hive of activity – a dozen assistants performing all manner of work, from slicing vegetables to washing dishes, took care of meals for the army of young wards and teaching staff under the watchful eye of the cook.

I smelled the characteristic aroma of curry, an exotic spice that formed the basis of the lunch being prepared, and which I'd become fond of during my time in India, where I'd served in the military for some years.

"Where were you stationed?" asked Riesling when I articulated my thoughts aloud.

"I was posted as an army doctor to the Fifth Northumberland Regiment in India, but when the second Afghan War began, I was reassigned to the Berkshire Regiment. After suffering an injury in the battle at Maiwand, I was moved to the Peshawar hospital, where I succumbed to a severe intestinal disease, ending my miliary career," I confided.

"I see," he nodded politely, and lost interest.

We paused only briefly in the kitchen. Holmes inquired whether Morgan had appeared the evening before and whether anybody had given her grape juice, but was unable to obtain any information other than that dinner had consisted of boiled beef. Nor were we able to determine Miss Davis's afternoon and evening whereabouts, and thereby her state of mind at day's end.

I was curious to see what direction Holmes would take from this dead end.

"Now let us have luncheon," the detective announced to my complete surprise, arranging with Riesling to meet again in the early afternoon, with headmaster Schaffer in attendance. "In the meantime, I shall set things straight in my mind, and hopefully have all the answers by then."

I was anything but hungry under the weight of the circumstances, but was prepared to accompany Holmes, whose appetite never seemed dulled by any agitation or oppression.

Yet he declined my company.

"I shall stop by the Diogenes Club to see my brother, as we have some matters to resolve," he apologised. "Besides, I perceive you have little appetite, Watson. Instead, I shall ask a favour of you. Go and see Haggins, who has surely examined Miss Morgan's corpse quite thoroughly by now. Ask him whether he noticed anything suspicious around the nose, or indeed ascertain it yourself. The rope the young lady hanged herself on should also be ready, so do bring it back."

He gave no further explanation, whistled for a cab and was gone.

I dutifully did all he asked of me, without knowing what purpose Haggins's findings would serve and how they might fit into the great detective's reasoning.

We met again some two and a half hours later, and were led directly to the headmaster's office.

Holmes had not returned in a good mood, so I supposed he had made no progress.

Schaffer and Riesling, both rather aloof, settled into their armchairs as we did, and waited for the detective to start speaking. Evidently, neither of them expected Holmes to identify the perpetrator of the torment which caused Lord Davis's daughter to take her life, and thought the whole affair would end up being swept under the rug without greater harm to the school's reputation.

But as always, my friend surprised them with his definite and uncompromising judgement.

"Regardless of what I've been told here today, it turns out that ordinary bullying among children is the least of the problems you may have to face," he opened his statement, firing off the rest like a gunshot. "For I have just reason to suspect that nothing of the kind was at play in this case. Miss Morgan was obscenely murdered!"

Schaffer gasped for breath and Riesling spat out the tea which he was sipping.

"Might I ask what makes you think so?" the headmaster inquired incredulously.

"Not only do I think so, but I am ready to reveal how the murder was committed, the motive and the murderer," Holmes replied coolly.

At that moment, one could have heard a pin drop in the room. Usually, Holmes savoured his monologues once he'd solved a case, but this time he was brusque. I attributed this to the age and innocence of the victim. He had no intention of exploiting this dramatic moment to exhibit his detective acumen.

"As soon as I saw the scene of the crime, it was obvious to me that the truth would differ greatly from what the murderer, should we accept my hypothesis, had attempted to make us believe. First and foremost, I do not believe that a slip of a girl, barefoot and nightgowned, would have been capable of climbing up to the lavatory ceiling, expertly tying the rope and then hanging herself on it, without any assistance."

Schaffer found nothing odd about it at all.

"Small children are as agile as monkeys, they can climb anywhere," he said with a wave of his hand.

"Then there is the length of the rope and the absence of a stool or chair to jump from," Holmes continued.

"I don't understand."

Holmes asked for my bag, from which he removed the rope I had retrieved from Haggins. "We shall of course have the height of the lavatories measured again, but it is obvious at first glance that the rope is too short for Morgan to have hanged herself from the toilet seat. She would have to have stood on something much higher – a chair or a stepladder. Yet nothing of the sort was found in the lavatories."

"Surely there is an explanation. Perhaps the maid or the doctor removed it."

"It cannot be explained," Holmes insisted. "Morgan simply could not have hanged herself on this length of rope and without some support under her feet, which nobody could have removed because it was never there. It is easily proven."

I had to admit that his logic was persuasive.

"But what about the farewell letter?" the headmaster exclaimed, starting from his armchair to remove the epistle from his drawer. "It is her writing, is it not?" he cried, waving the letter about.

Holmes nodded, but did not consider it irrefutable evidence.

"The letter is indeed authentic, but it has been manipulated," he announced.

"Somebody forced her to write it?" the deputy asked, raising his eyebrows. "You must be fantasising. I suggest we call for a graphologist, who will surely give us the truth. As far as I know, it will be easy to determine whether Morgan wrote the letter of her own will or under duress."

"An analysis shall be most welcome," smiled the detective, but it was the sly smile of a cobra, inconspicuously approaching its chosen prey. "Do you know what such an analysis would determine, above all? That the ink is three years old."

I understood. "Is it the letter she wrote during her first attempt at suicide?"

"Not first, but only attempt," Holmes corrected me. "The murderer merely used the letter to help conceal his heinous crime and disguise it as another, unfortunately successful attempt. Notice how close to the upper edge of the paper the writing begins – there is almost no natural margin. The paper was trimmed to remove the upper section, which doubtless contained the date."

The two pedagogues were sorting his words in their heads.

"In the context of the school, her mention of mistreatment might, when cleverly interpreted, suggest bullying from the other girls, but in my opinion she meant nothing of the kind. You may consider this part of my investigative conclusions to be good news."

Neither Schaffer nor Riesling looked especially delighted.

"Now wait... How do you explain that a letter dating back three years and of such a sensitive nature would find its way into the hands of your imaginary murderer?" asked the headmaster, hesitant to believe.

"I shall get to that promptly, along with the motive," the detective assured him.

"I simply don't believe it," fidgeted Riesling. "Just the question of how to plan a murder of this sort. Are you suggesting somebody abducted the little girl from her bedroom in the night and dragged her to the lavatory? Why, she was there sleeping with the other girls! She would surely have made a fuss and woken the others!"

My friend's mind was firm even in this regard.

"The murderer was quite familiar with how the school is run. He knew that the wards of the St. Ignatius Catholic School are almost always under supervision – either of the teachers, the house mistresses or the children themselves. He had practically no opportunity to attack, so he had to wait for Morgan to come to him. Or rather, to go to the lavatory alone in the night."

Riesling threw up his hands gleefully. "Why, surely Mr. Holmes, you must see what nonsense you are trying to persuade us of. So the murderer hid in the lavatories for heaven knows how long, waiting for Morgan to come in there alone at night? It's absurd! What if a different girl had appeared? Or did he not care who it was? One cannot plan something of the sort, I beg you!"

"Mr. Riesling, you teach biology, if I am not mistaken?" the detective continued, undeterred. "So you must surely be familiar with the effects of sweetened beverages. They are diuretic. And why? Because they contain excess sugar, which the body instantly eliminates through urine. If you wish to force somebody go to the toilet in the night, give them a sweet juice before bed."

As a physician, I had to admit Holmes was right. "And somebody had given Morgan a jug of grape juice before bed!" I recalled. "He could easily have estimated at what time the urge would coax the girl to get up. But who? And why?"

Schaffer slumped miserably in his armchair, no longer looking quite so stubborn.

"Why indeed?" he repeated desperately. "Why would anybody do something of the sort?"

"This is the crucial question, which we have finally circled back to. The fundamental essence of every crime – the motive!" exclaimed Holmes, raising his forefinger and piercing the air before him with it.

Even I could no longer breathe for excitement.

"I have spent the last two hours with my brother Mycroft, who holds a very high position in our esteemed government, as you all know," he confided. "As such, he has access to any variety of information, or is at least able to procure it."

While speaking, he pulled a watch from his waistcoat pocket and checked the time.

"When he asked me to look into poor Morgan's case this morning, he did so knowing that she was the daughter of Thomas Davis, a respected member of the House of Lords. However, Lord Davis has been gravely ill for some time, and his son, Stewart, is expected to inherit both his title and his fortune within the next few months. And because my brother is rather insightful, he had young master Stewart investigated this very morning. By lunchtime, he had received the report. It would seem that the fortune he is to share with his sister, Morgan. upon their father's death would scarcely cover his gambling debts. He needed her portion as well."

"Are you suggesting that he had his sister killed so as to become the sole heir?" I asked, horrified.

"Everything suggests it. It was he who gave the murderer her old farewell letter, and plotted and staged it all. Evidently, he was never particularly fond of his sister, for he is the person she writes of in the letter, the one who mistreated and abused her. Morgan was tormented by her own adult brother. Stewart never showed any interest in her, and it was he who persuaded their father to send her to boarding school."

Holmes glanced at his watch again.

"Excellent," he murmured contentedly. "Our friends from Scotland Yard will have arrived at the Davis estate by now, and master Stewart will surely be answering their questions shortly."

"He may even confide who the hired killer is," I said hopefully.

"But my dear Watson, I already know," the detective said, depositing the watch in his pocket and looking intently at Schaffer's deputy, Riesling. "Let us call a spade a spade, shall we?"

The deputy paled and his perfect façade seemed to lose some of its sleekness.

"What are you saying?" he said, clearing his throat.

"I am merely saying that you are the wolf in sheep's clothing, and one of the most hideous murderers I have ever met," Holmes retorted to his face.

"What evidence have you for such accusations?"

"Oh, it was quite elementary," remarked the detective, crossing his legs in the armchair. "From the moment I first saw you, I knew you must be a former soldier. Your bearing, your attention to dress and manner – the drill of the military oozes from every pore of your body. Yet later in the kitchen, after you reacted so coolly to learning that my friend Watson is also a former soldier, I corrected my opinion. The rivalry between the infantry and the Royal Navy is common knowledge, so I judged that you had trained and served in the latter. And you yourself told me that it was you who had given headmaster Schaffer the – as you called it – discovered farewell letter. It was you who instilled the idea that the writer was speaking of torment, and in his shock, the headmaster accepted your claim without hesitation."

Riesling rose slowly, but Holmes remained calmly seated. I regretted not having brought my trusty old revolver, but never would I have thought it would be needed on school grounds. Yet the detective utterly ignored the deputy, who was exuding a silent menace.

"As I hinted earlier, it was you who gave Morgan the sweet juice before bed, and then you waited for her in the lavatory. Had anybody else come in before her, you would simply have remained hidden in one of the stalls. Apropos, Watson," he turned to me. "Did Haggins obtain the information I inquired about?"

"Yes, Morgan had light burn injuries in her nose," I admitted in a daze.

"Aha! I was not mistaken about that either," Holmes thanked me for the news. "So, Mr. Riesling, you ambushed her and subdued her with chloroform. Then it took little effort to slip her body into the noose and unscrupulously hang the poor girl."

As he spoke, Schaffer stepped as far away from his deputy as possible, blinking his eyes fearfully.

Riesling looked ready to pounce on the detective.

"At first, I was unable to explain to myself why you would do such a thing, but Mycroft proved helpful in this regard as well. He is far more clever than I! He discovered that you had served in the Royal Navy with Stewart Davis, so you knew each other well, but you also shared the vice of gambling. With your meagre teacher's wage, you were even worse off than your noble friend, so his plan suited you remarkably well," concluded Holmes.

The recess bell rang, and girlish giggles echoed from the door separating the headmaster's office from the school corridor. We were three of us facing Riesling, but Schaffer and I were no match for his physical prowess, and I'm afraid the former sailor would have overcome even the strong and agile detective.

A police whistle sounded below the windows opening onto the street. It was coming closer.

"Two squads have departed from the Yard, that is obvious," Holmes met the deputy's gaze.

Riesling glared back into his steel grey eyes, countless options likely filling his head.

Then his gaze flitted to the fireplace, adorned with a cavalry sabre on the mantle.

"As a solider, you have only one recourse, Mr. Riesling. I shall not stop you," Holmes said curtly.

The deputy headmaster took several deep breaths as he fought with himself, and then gave us a salute.

His death was mentioned only briefly in the newspapers, overshadowed by the much greater tragedy.

THE ADVENTURE OF THE INTERCHANGED KEY

I must grant significant, perhaps even the most significant merit for the fame and reputation of my friend, Sherlock Holmes to my esteemed literary agent, Sir Arthur Conan Doyle. It was he who managed all my publication efforts, be they in journals, magazines or books. Alongside Holmes, he was my first critic, advisor, editor of our adventures, and it was he who often helped me select the great detective's cases even before I began writing, so as to choose those that would appeal to and surprise the public with a sufficiently original plot. I always get chills when I realise how many excellent literary crime stories were shelved due to secondary circumstances – the social or political context of the time, the need for concealment in the interest of the security of the British Empire* or simply because the persons involved did not wish for them to be publicised.

I did, however, manage to deal with the latter issue by slightly altering the circumstances and names, and sometimes even the dates and locations, enough to ensure that the real persons would have no reason to be upset, while preserving a proper depiction of Holmes's procedures without detracting from his deductive abilities. Mr. Doyle supported me in this "amendment of the truth," driven naturally by his interest as a literary agent. "There is no need to ruin a good story with excessive realism," he often assured me, while we were seeking ways to publish some sensitive document or other.

I was therefore surprised by the utterly different attitude he assumed when, for once, he himself was at the centrepoint of our investigation. At the time, he was determined that absolutely nothing about the affair should come to light, for an agent of respectable literature cannot afford similar embarrassment, and it might even be detrimental to my own work.

But much water has passed under the bridge since then.

Today, so many years later, I see no reason not to commit my memories to paper, especially as this adventure is indeed among the most curious. A murder among the ranks of detective novel writers certainly seems so to me.

Late one evening, around the turn of the century, Holmes and I were disturbed in our rooms by a messenger who would not be denied entry, claiming he had an urgent missive from Mr. Doyle himself. Besides the hour, which did not suggest a work issue, the fact that the otherwise distinguished gentleman would choose this form of communication unsettled me. In the handwritten note, he asked whether Holmes and I would come immediately to the address of a hotel in Lambeth.

"Given the tone and the speed at which he must have scribbled the message, I suppose it must be something urgent," the detective observed after briefly examining the note. "His writing is shaky, the individual words are barely in a straight line, and he even misspelled something. Yet, instead of rewriting the message, he simply crossed out the mistake. There is no doubt Mr. Doyle is greatly distressed."

Holmes took very little convincing.

While we dressed hurriedly, the waiting messenger hailed a cab, and we were soon dashing through Mayfair and Belgravia towards Lambeth Bridge over the Thames.

"I would have thought your scribbling earned rather more money. The hotel Doyle has summoned us to is not among the finest. Indeed, I would expect to find someone of the lower middle class there," he pondered as the carriage meandered through the thinning traffic.

To the best of my knowledge, my agent's offices were located somewhere entirely different, nor was his private residence anywhere in the vicinity, so I merely shrugged. The impertinent remark concerning my writing fees, which had never been my chief source of income, I chose to overlook. Unfortunately, I did share my friend's surprise as to what Doyle could be doing in a place such as this. I couldn't avoid the suspicion that the respectable gentleman may have let himself go with a young lady, found a love nest in a cheap hotel, and something had happened.

I could sense a scandal brewing.

Having arrived at the spot, we found our assumptions to be correct. It was a shabby brick building with dusty windows, most of them drowning in darkness. In only a few, a faint light shone from behind heavy curtains, attracting moths. The pavement was empty. We stepped quickly inside and past the abandoned reception desk, with a bell on the counter and a sign indicating that the receptionist was available on call. This came as little surprise – it was indeed a place where it was advisable not to check who was coming and going, better not to see or hear them. We headed upstairs on the worn red carpet to the room whose number the messenger had given before disappearing.

Mr. Doyle was not in the company of a young lady, but rather a man.

He was lying prostrate on the floor in the middle of the room, quite dead. The cause of his demise was undoubtedly the splinter fracture at the crown of his skull, which was bleeding profusely. Had I been called in as a doctor, we would have arrived too late.

The expression on my face must have been full of questions. Doyle, waiting for us in a chair near a writing desk beneath the darkened window, rose instantly and blurted out an answer to the most crucial of these.

"I didn't kill him," he said firmly, but with visible concern. "I found him like this!"

The good old soul, who conveys my work to readers, was a heap of misfortune. Attired in a tweed suit with a green cravat and snowy white collar, he looked quite out of place in the drab room, considering the circumstances.

"With all due respect, I've heard countless assurances of the kind in my career, not all of them based on the truth. Please, do allow me to judge for myself, freely and without prejudice," Holmes retorted, rather unfeelingly.

"But gentlemen, we know each other intimately! Why Doctor, you cannot possibly believe…" Doyle gasped.

"It is of no consequence what we believe, but what the clues and evidence lead us to," the detective interrupted him, preventing me from rushing forward to reassure my friend. Even he remained standing just inside the door, so as not to trample on any clues, systematically scanning the room with his gaze. "What have you touched in here?"

"Nothing," the agent proffered. "As soon as I stepped in and saw what had happened, I called for a messenger and passed him the note for you through a crack in the door. Not even he knows why I sent for you. Good God, this could ruin me!"

"Allow me to correct you," my friend chided him brusquely. "At the very least, you touched the pen, the pad of paper, the chair you are seated on, the door handle and the doorframe."

Doyle's large, twisted moustache, protruding to both sides, drooped suddenly and sweat beaded on his lofty brow.

He began muttering something, but Holmes cut him off with an annoyed wave of the hand.

"Your behaviour was far from exemplary for a publisher of detective stories," he uttered. Holmes stepped towards the publisher and grasped his palms in his own. Had the latter interpreted this as a gesture of apology or assurance that all would be well, he was quite mistaken.

My friend drew Doyle's hands up close to his face, as though to kiss them, and started examining them minutely, even taking out his obligatory magnifying glass for assistance, and topping off this performance by sniffing at the skin.

"I say! I must protest!" the suspect exclaimed indignantly.

"If you desire my help, you will have to endure my methods," the detective retorted, proceeding to roll up Doyle's jacket sleeves. Only then was he satisfied. "I believe you," he added more gently.

"What was that charade supposed to mean?"

"I had to be certain," Holmes explained. "Nevertheless, I admit that your perfectly manicured hands committed no violent crime, at least not in the past several days. Nor do your spotless cuffs bear any traces of blood, which would be an inevitable consequence of so brutal an act," the detective motioned towards the dead man.

"Why, the murderer would not have sent for you himself…"

"You might be surprised," reacted the detective with a mysterious expression, but he did not elaborate on his remark.

Instead, he turned his attention to the victim.

"I suppose you know the poor fellow?" I asked Doyle, while Holmes examined the corpse. "Can you tell us who he is?"

Doyle nodded.

"His name is… his name was Fred. He worked for me and my publishing house. I was to collect a finished order here tonight."

"A writer?"

"Not at all. Fred was… a book doctor."

I had never heard the term before. "The man was a doctor?" I said, bemused.

Doyle shook his head. "In our business, a book doctor is somebody who analyses manuscripts and pinpoints why they do not work and how to improve them," he explained. "Be it to your credit, Doctor Watson, that you have never encountered one. But publishers often employ them, albeit I have yet to meet a writer who would admit it. Imagine the blow to their ego – struggling with a manuscript that simply refuses to come out right. A book doctor can often salvage it. You'd be surprised how many of today's bestsellers and famous authors owe their success to the intervention of just such anonymous helpers as Fred here was…"

I could hardly be surprised that Doyle would not receive such a person at his office, but instead met him somewhere where they would not be seen. It had to remain a secret, as did the illusionary genius of Doyle's authors.

"Then my supposition that Fred's death is directly linked to his occupation need not be entirely outlandish. It certainly doesn't look like a random robbery," Holmes said, raising his eyes from the corpse and gazing at the murder weapon.

I, too, had noticed it immediately upon our arrival.

The large, heavy, black metal Remington typewriter could hardly be overlooked.

The dead man was lying in a pool of blood not far from it, one cramped arm still outstretched to the keys, as though he had attempted to continue working until his last breath …

Doyle frowned. "Writers may be vain, but in the end they have the final veto. Neither Fred nor I enforced any interventions in their work. If they insisted on disregarding Fred's amendments, the worst that could happen would be that they would take back their manuscript and offer it to another agent. I can see no motive for murder here…"

My own experience with Arthur Conan Doyle was quite the same. We had often argued over certain changes to my texts, but he never pressed me to accept them, and our collaboration was based on dialogue.

"What commissions was Fred currently working on," Holmes inquired.

Doyle hesitated for a moment, but when we promised not to divulge which of his promising authors required such uncharacteristic assistance, he relented.

"Fred was working on two manuscripts. One for a successful author of women's novels, Miss Yvonne Fairchild; the second, an adventure novel by Adam Zembalista. Adam is one of the mainstays of our publishing house!"

Even I had heard of this young author, although I was not among his readers. All the same, successful novels set among the European aristocracy allegedly offered just the right mix of historical fact, romantic suspense, intrigue and subterfuge.

"Sadly, in recent months Adam seemed to be struggling with some form of writer's block, and Fred quite literally plucked a thorn from his side with his fresh ideas in his last book," Doyle added. "One might entertain the idea that Adam had wanted to get rid of a witness to his disgrace, but that would require killing several other people who are privy to the matter, including myself. Besides, Adam is on the verge of completing another novel, and I don't know how he will manage without Fred. Even if I were to concede that Adam could be capable of such a thing, which I don't believe he is, the murder would work against him."

The detective made no comment on Doyle's deduction and turned the man's body onto its back.

He was a rather handsome man with Slavic features, fair hair and a moustache, his lifeless blue eyes now fixed rigidly on nothing.

"Hullo, hullo!" Holmes suddenly rejoiced over the corpse.

A long, fair hair was curled around the dead man's trouser leg. My friend grasped it carefully and held it up to the light. "Undoubtedly a woman's, freshly washed and curled," he concluded.

"I hate to admit it, but Miss Fairchild has blonde hair," the publisher said grimly.

"Whose manuscript was Fred supposed to turn in today? Which one did you come to collect?"

"*Lily, Maid in Piccadilly*," Doyle blushed, muttering something to the effect that romance novels had seen unprecedented commercial success in recent years.

"What is Miss Fairchild's physical constitution," continued the detective, shifting his attention to the murder weapon. "It would take considerable strength to lift such a typewriter, which weighs many pounds, and strike someone over the head with it…"

"If it were a murder in the heat of the moment, even a slight person can exert surprising abilities for a short amount of time," I said, searching for a possible explanation.

"She is of slight stature…" the publisher admitted haltingly. "But I have seen her angry before, and have no desire to experience her spewing fire again."

From my point of view, everything fell into place beautifully.

"I should think that if we pay a visit to Miss Fairchild's home, everything will be quite clear. Surely, she won't deny it for long, and will tell us what happened here, and why," I proposed, imagining that in the end, the investigation would not be very difficult, and I might hope to get to bed at a decent hour.

The bells outside were already striking midnight, the time when a gentleman pours his last glass of sherry.

Yet Holmes seemed disinclined to leave. "Perhaps," he murmured. What could still be on his mind?

"How long has Fred been in your employ?" he asked Doyle after a while.

"Several years now."

"What do you know of his personal life? Where is he from?"

"He was not a gregarious man…" admitted Doyle. "Truth be told, I know very little about his past. He was recommended by an editor from the Strand, and his skills and willingness to remain silent were more important to me, so I never really inquired. He had an accent I couldn't place, but he certainly wasn't a Londoner."

Holmes scratched his chin and looked around again.

"Speaking of which, where is the novel then? You said you hadn't touched anything!"

The publisher threw up his hands. "There is no manuscript here. I don't know where it is."

"Nor do I see any papers, there is nothing in the basket or in the typewriter," Holmes surveyed the bloodied machine once more with his magnifying glass. "Curious. Even the typewriting ribbon is gone. Fred could not have removed it, because his fingers would have been covered in ink, which they are not. The perpetrator must have done it."

"The lady most likely simply took the manuscript with her," Doyle suggested. "Surely we will find it at her home, which will only serve as further evidence."

Yet the detective continued to stall.

"Watson, do you not find the position we found him in suspicious?"

"You mean the arm outstretched to the typewriter?" I understood what he was suggesting.

He nodded. "Fred seems to have lived for a few moments after the blow. He was writhing. Perhaps, in the

36

delirium caused by the brain contusion, he attempted to reach for the typewriter and type a message. But before escaping, the culprit preventively removed any paper from within the reach of the prostrate body, and took out the ink tape for good measure. Look, there is a small scrap left in the paper holder where the murderer tore it out. But he didn't bother with the note pad on the desk, being quite sure that the fatally injured and dying man would never reach it."

"Why didn't he simply take the typewriter away?"

"Dragging off a heavy machine is far more laborious than simply taking out the paper and tape. Or perhaps he wanted to avoid making more noise. Or he may have been disturbed."

"Or she had no strength left," remarked Doyle, turning attention back to the lady writer.

"It is starting to look more like premediated murder than a spur of the moment crime!" I exclaimed.

"It may be a combination of both. The killer acted on impulse, but once the crime was committed, he started covering his tracks. Or she," the detective finally admitted what seemed most probable to Doyle and me.

We had encountered many charming angels of death before today.

"A pity that the murderer was so cold-blooded and thought of everything," I sighed.

Holmes, still examining the typewriter, grew alert.

"Perhaps not everything," he hissed excitedly, peering at the Remington again through the magnifying glass. "He removed the tape, but the 'second ink' will give us a clue nonetheless!"

Doyle and I looked at each other quizzically.

"What ink?" I ventured to ask, dreading the answer.

"Blood, Watson! Fred pointed at his killer with his own blood!"

From my vantage point, the entire keyboard of the typewriter seemed spattered with blood.

I remarked this to my friend, who gave me his usual compassionate look, the one he reserved for those moments when he found me particularly inept.

"Yes, it is precisely because the machine is covered in blood that we can read the keyboard… well, like a book. Fred's fingers are likewise covered in blood, which I initially ascribed to his having touched his wound. But I think he was reaching for the typewriter and grasping at the keys. He was unable to put anything to paper, but was trying with all his remaining might to press a single key. In doing so, he smudged the drop of blood on it."

As always, Holmes was right. How could I have missed it! One letter on the splattered keyboard was partly smudged. It was the Y key.

Yvonne Fairchild had clearly failed to think of that.

Doyle rubbed his face wearily. "Well then… Good heavens… Gentlemen, act as you see fit, but in the strictest confidentiality, I beg you. Above all, no press. I will attempt to have a statement ready by morning."

"No need to hurry yet," the detective restrained him. "Before I have Miss Fairchild arrested, I will need two more things. The first is an older manuscript that Fred had worked on previously. Surely you will have some at your office," he asked the agent, "Furthermore, your contract with Fred, which I am sure bears his initials, and may give me some answers. Ideally, if you could get both immediately and have them delivered to me at our suspect's address. Watson and I will make our way there in the meantime."

"She is most likely the murderer, but if Mr. Doyle wishes to avoid a scandal, do you think we will be received without a fuss at this time of night?" I objected.

"It is Friday, my dear friend," Holmes laughed. "And you are the only artist I know who goes to bed before midnight. And if indeed you are right, Miss Yvonne will have plenty of adrenaline in her blood after the murder, and will not retire to bed anytime soon."

Sir Arthur Conan Doyle, only too glad to leave the room of horror, obediently departed, as did I and the detective, but not before locking and thoroughly sealing off the room and waking the night porter in the cubicle behind the reception desk. The drunken wretch had not even noticed us moving about the hotel, let alone having any inkling of what had occurred upstairs.

After a brief interrogation, which merely affirmed our suspicion that he had not seen anybody come in or out of the building, Holmes ordered him not to let anybody into Mr.

Fred's room on any pretext, until we or the police patrol returned. We then carried on to Miss Fairchild's quarters, which were fortunately also located in central London.

My friend had been correct in assuming she would not be asleep.

On the contrary, there was a party on at her luxurious home. Indeed, we had very little trouble getting inside – the butler opened the door and despite our ordinary clothes, he assumed we were among the invited guests. In artistic circles, appropriate attire is not so great a matter of concern.

The drawing room was bathed in white light from crystal chandeliers and there was loud music mingled with the throaty laughter emanating from dozens of exuberant guests at the height of entertainment.

In the midst of a group of gentleman, most in coattails, stood a petite lady, some years past her prime, dressed in a black sequined dress with an ostrich feather woven into her swept-up hair.

Holmes lost no time in joining the group. He laughed theatrically at some witticism or other, then kissed the hostess's hand and asked her for a word in private, where I joined them. Her initial confusion, being unable to place our faces and instead pretending we were acquainted to avoid a faux pas, turned into indignation as soon as she found out we had intruded on her *soirée* as strangers.

"Gentlemen, I cannot fathom what sort of impertinence has induced you to such an outrageous act," she fumed.

"You will see soon enough, madam, and I am sure you will forgive me, but I must ask you a few questions. Know that we are here on official business, and it is very urgent indeed."

Miss Yvonne seated herself gracefully in a leather armchair in her study, and invited the detective to ask his questions. I observed her expression when he told her of Fred's death, but her surprise may have merely been a well-studied act.

"Before I carry on, I should warn you that Mr. Doyle has confessed to us the nature of your cooperation with Fred, so there is no need to conceal anything," concluded Holmes.

Miss Fairchild raised her eyebrows and took a long drag from her pearl-tipped cigarette.

"I see," she said. "I do hope I can rely on your discretion."

"As long as you answer truthfully, you have nothing to fear."

I wondered why my friend was conducting the interrogation with such tact, and waited anxiously to see what would come of it. In his place, I would have been done with it in a heartbeat.

"Did you visit Fred at his lodgings today?"

"I won't deny it. It was an appointment arranged some days ago."

"Because of your manuscript?"

"Naturally, why else? They may still title me as Miss, but I am of an age when I am far more interested in my begonias than pleasures of the flesh."

I had to smile at her self-deprecation, which I found appealing.

"What state was the manuscript in?"

"Untouched. Fred told me that he hadn't even started working on it yet," she shrugged. "He said that he would inform Mr. Doyle to that effect later today. He apologised, saying I should not take it personally, but that he had made a personal decision concerning his career, and would no longer have time for my texts."

"What decision was that?"

"He didn't say."

Inwardly, I delighted in how cleverly Holmes had extracted the motive for murder from the woman.

"Did you kill him?" Holmes asked directly.

She laughed. "Are you mad? Why would I do that? I wished him good luck!"

"You took your manuscript with you?"

"Yes, it's here somewhere," she motioned her hand with the cigarette towards the polished wooden bureau. "I haven't yet decided what to do with it. I shall consult Mr. Doyle."

"Might I see it?"

Miss Fairchild made no objection, opened the drawer and handed my friend a stack of densely lettered sheets. "I'm not sure it is your type of reading…"

He gave them a cursory glance. "One must not be disdainful of anything. I need to borrow one sheet. May I? I assume you wrote all of them yourself?"

"Why certainly. They were written in this room on a typewriter locked in the cabinet. Would you like to see it?" she offered with undisguised sarcasm.

"That will not be necessary at present," the detective thanked her, folding a single sheet into his pocket. "We won't detain you from your company any longer. I wish you a pleasant evening."

We bid a polite farewell to the ageing miss and allowed ourselves to be shown out.

I followed Holmes, who was quite calm, out of the house, utterly consternated that he hadn't arrested her, or even accused her of the murder. He seemed to believe her.

As if on cue, Doyle's carriage bearing a sleepy assistant drew up in front of the building to deliver an envelope with the documents the detective had requested.

He opened it swiftly and perused the papers.

"Ha! Just as I expected!" he exclaimed with satisfaction. "Watson, we can now make an arrest!"

Relief washed over me – we were acting on certainty after all. But instead of returning the house, Holmes stepped into the carriage, waiting for me to follow.

"I don't understand… are we not going to arrest Miss Fairchild? You just said …"

"…that we are going to make an arrest. But not Miss Fairchild. I never really suspected her. Come now, you could be in bed soon," he urged me impatiently. "I promise to explain everything in minute detail later."

He ordered the coachman to drive us to the address of Adam Zembalista.

I sat stunned in the carriage, striving to put together the fragments of all I had seen to fit Holmes's conviction that Zembalista was the murderer. I had failed to keep up with his logic throughout most of our friendship, but was often able, retrospectively, to sort many things out in my mind. Not this time.

"And yet, it was elementary, my dear Watson," said the detective, amused by my reticence, which he rightfully attributed to the chaos in my head. "When you have two suspects and one can be eliminated with absolute certainty, then it must be the other."

"But all the evidence pointed at Yvonne Fairchild, did it not?"

"You mean the hair?" he suggested. "She admitted to having been there. The missing manuscript? No mystery there, she simply took it with her. Unlike you, I only found evidence to show she could not have done it. Think along with me, my dear chap," he challenged.

I waited anxiously for his speech.

"Firstly, the blow to Fred's head," he began. "Fred was considerably taller than Miss Fairchild, and the blow struck at an angle, which simply does not correspond to her stature, regardless of any emotion. He was killed by somebody of at least equal height. It was not your good Mr. Doyle. Secondly, you know only too well how difficult it is to wash off typewriter ink when you stain yourself. You have been struggling with it ever since I've known you. The killer handled the ink tape, which is impossible without leaving stains. When I kissed Miss Fairchild's hand, I couldn't find the slightest trace of ink. I could go on."

But I had at least one counter-argument.

"And how do you explain the smudged blood on the Y key? You concluded yourself that Fred was attempting to identify his killer. Y for Yvonne, what else could it me? There is no 'y' in the name Zembalista!"

"This did puzzle me for a few minutes," the detective admitted. "But this, too, has a simple explanation. Indeed, it is confirmed by Mr. Doyle's reports," he said, handing me the envelope.

I opened it and perceived several pages of another manuscript, and Fred's contract.

"To understand what I am getting at, allow me a brief excursion," Holmes settled into the carriage seat across from me. "The layout of letters on keyboards has a fascinating history. Originally, the sequence of keys was not uniform on all typewriters. But in the last roughly twenty years,** manufacturers have standardised what is known as the Q, W, E, R, T, Y arrangement, according to the order of the keys from left to right on the first row of the keyboard. It was only in 1888, at a convention of experts in Toronto, that this layout was declared universal! And therein lies the rub," he said, preparing to lay out his trump card.

"Although Fred had a perfect a command of the language of Shakespeare, that is, English – indeed so good that he could write in it – he was originally from the Austro-Hungarian Empire. According to his contract, his name was Fred Hammerschmidt, a Viennese Bohemian whose native tongue was German. And there it is. German typewriters have one sole difference in their layout. The Y and Z keys are interchanged. In German texts, the letter 'z' occurs more frequently, and therefore it has a more exclusive position. Before coming to England, Fred had learned to type on a Q, W, E, R, T, Z keyboard."

I smacked my palm against my forehead.

"At death's door, with an injury to his brain, he must have subconsciously switched to his mother tongue. He automatically reached for the letter 'y', but he meant 'z'," I added. "Z for Zembalista, his killer."

"Quite so," Holmes confirmed. "I proceeded with this conviction, but it took me some time to find a motive. Now, however, I am quite certain of it. In a moment we shall find out whether I was right or wrong."

Adam Zembalista confessed almost forthwith. We found him at home in a state of nervous breakdown, his hands stained not only with ink, but also with blood.

Nor was Holmes mistaken about the motive. While still in the carriage, he outlined his reasoning, which was incited by

Miss Fairchild. Fred was indeed planning to change his occupation. No longer wanting to be an anonymous shadow, he yearned for recognition and his own name on the covers of books. Just as he had returned her manuscript to Yvonne, he had returned Zembalista's, who had been drawing not only on Fred's ideas, but also on his knowledge of the European noble families he wrote about.

The mistake that had cost Fred his life was to boast to Zembalista about his own new work.

The jealous and embittered author, who would thereby have lost the only chance of retaining his reputation and the financial reward that went with it, lost control and murdered his rival on the spot in a fit of rage, stealing the manuscript at the same time.

For in Zembalista's study we found not only the manuscript Fred had returned, but another brand new one. Despite Zembalista's name emblazoned on the title page, he could not have been the author, as demonstrated by Holmes through a comparative analysis of the three manuscripts he had gathered that evening.

"Every typewriter has a unique cast of letters, which have minor flaws and discrepancies. No two typewriters make the same imprint," he instructed me. "Doyle gave me an old manuscript that Fred had retyped on his machine. It is identical to the one Zembalista hoped to pass off as his own. He authentic work, like that of Miss Fairchild, was demonstrably written on an entirely different typewriter."

I was a long time falling asleep that night, and for the next several months I once again recorded our adventures the old-fashioned way – with a fountain pen.

* Today, we know that Watson nevertheless wrote down a number of these adventures and hid them in various places, where they are continuously being found by his heirs.

** Our story is set around the year 1900.

THE ADVENTURE OF THE

TULIPS ON ICE

The disparate array of expertise in numerous fields of human knowledge was one of the things that never ceased to fascinate me about my friend Sherlock Holmes. In some areas his knowledge bordered on encyclopaedic, while at others he groped like a novice. Yet he continued to learn all his life. As I have doubtless recounted many times before, his chief field of study was chemistry – indeed, our quarters at 221B Baker Street were full of various flasks, tubes, burners and myriad other equipment that would put many a laboratory in Oxford to shame. In time, I became accustomed to the odours emanating from his kit in the drawing room, and after a most unpleasant blunder one morning, I began taking considerable care as to which jar I spooned sugar from to sweeten my tea.

Nor am I acquainted with anyone else who, merely by analysing a small heap of cigar ash that had fallen onto a hall rug, could with such certainty identify the mysterious visitor at Lord Straford's manor house, promptly leading to the identification of his killer. A monograph Holmes had written on the subject had become quite well-known even outside professional circles. Yet his interests reached far beyond this. He naturally had an excellent understanding of biology and anthropology, and could almost outdo me in medicine, but surely none of this comes as a surprise to regular readers of the *Strand* magazine and the adventures of this paragon of modern criminal science.

Recently, however, certain circumstances recalled to my mind a case which was marginal in essence, and which I originally had no intention of putting on record, but on which I would presently like to demonstrate how capable Holmes was of impressing me time and again, even after years of collaboration.

It occurred at a point when we had been residing at his farm at *Cuckmere Haven* in Sussex for some time, enjoying our retirement. Holmes was chiefly engaged in beekeeping, while I caught up on the piles of literature I hadn't had time to read during my hectic life. Precious little could draw us out of our contented rural shell.

All the same, we could not refuse an invitation to celebrate the birthday of our dear Mrs. Hudson. By then, our former landlady of many years was living permanently with her younger sister, who cared for the good woman in her advanced age with the same solicitude that the landlady had bestowed on us for most of her life. Devotion seemingly ran in the Hudson family, and we could only hope that the proverbial art of cookery was likewise hereditary.

Fortunately, the ladies lived at no great distance. Comfortably ensconced in the compartment of a local train, which ran along the high cliffs of Dover before plunging into endless pastures crossed by meandering rivers, the detective and I guessed whether lunch would consist of beef or fish, the preparation of which our landlady had always excelled at. Holmes then opened a newspaper and dived into it with relish. It is a well-known fact that he adored tabloids, with all their passion, emotions and scandals. On the other hand, he described my preferred *Daily Telegraph* as reading for staid intellectuals, and found it utterly uninteresting.

"That is no newspaper for ordinary folk," he would say. "They live for events in their immediate proximity, while rags like that one scorn the everyday lives of the majority of this nation. Instead, they focus on geopolitics or squabbles in the House of Lords. Nothing could be further removed from our butcher on the corner."

I had no intention of letting him spoil my regular ritual. Moreover, I found he was mistaken this time, because most of the newspapers were focused on the health of King Edward, who had come down with bronchitis earlier in the year in Paris, and the general opinion was that his condition was unfavourable. He had days, perhaps weeks to live. And nobody could be indifferent to the fate of the monarch, indeed of Great Britain, be they an intellectual or a cook.

But there was no sense arguing with Holmes. Over the edge of the paper, I saw his bright eyes devouring each line with gusto. I could only surmise what he was reading from the headlines on the front page, which revolved almost masochistically around the case of Doctor Crippen, who had poisoned his wife and buried her body in the cellar of their London home, and the gas explosion at Wellington Colliery in Whitehaven that had killed 136 people.

Every now and then, my concentration was disturbed by Holmes's ejaculations, torn out of any comprehensible context. "They've only known each other a week!" he exclaimed indignantly, then a moment later, with some surprise, he observed that "she couldn't have been that old." I had just been reading the obituary of the Italian painter

Francesco Monachesi, who had succumbed to a protracted illness in Rome at the age of ninety-three, and recalling our journey to the Italian capital, when the exasperated detective finally sought my attention directly.

"Behold, Watson. This is precisely what I mean!" he exclaimed, shoving an article from his paper under my nose and demanding attention, heedless of my annoyance. "A series of robberies among small tradesmen across the county. The loot is never big enough to excite the police inspectors or local government, yet it is devastating to the victims. But since there is no promotion to be gained from such minor investigations, and more than a year remains until the municipal elections, the authorities are lax. But locals fearing for their livelihoods, ending up in poorhouses with their entire families, is not plump enough a morsel for your illustrious *Times*."

Indeed, a fairly large section of one of the tabloids was filled with the lamentations of a baker, a confectioner and a tobacconist, for whom the stolen sales meant existential difficulties. The *modus operandi* was always the same. There were always two assailants – one of smaller stature, the other bulky – who lay in ambush, waiting until the victim was quite alone. The only mitigating circumstance was that they left no corpses.

"I should think it is understandable," I retorted, "at least in terms of journalistic approach. Why, the major newspapers cannot possibly concern themselves with every minor incident, of which there must be hundreds across the nation. Which is precisely what makes them a topic for these local journals," I shrugged, pushing away the newspaper. "But

I agree that the disregard on the part of the authorities is reprehensible."

Holmes snorted angrily, as always when the conversation turned to the abilities of the state police. With some rare exceptions, he considered the members of the force to be an incompetent lot, often impeding rather than aiding investigations with their idiocy. He had little patience even for the legends of Scotland Yard honoured with a Victoria Medal, like Lestrade or Phibs.

"It is sheer incompetence!" he fumed. His grey brain cells, accustomed to activity, unable to rest when presented with a problem until they had solved the puzzle, must have been suffering. "Where is the analysis of clues at the scene? Where are the informants? The culprits must be disposing of the loot with dealers and usurers. They should have been questioned and stopped long ago!"

I could hardly object to any of this, and we spent the remainder of the journey in silence.

A short time later, we were standing on the platform of a small village railway station, with clouds of steam billowing around our legs. It was not far to the Hudsons' house from here, but I was not inclined to walk.

I noticed Holmes looking about curiously.

"Are you looking for a cab?" I asked with relief that we were of one mind. "Surely we can hire one in front of the inn."

"Yes, yes, Watson, I know. But I realised something else. We cannot arrive emptyhanded!"

I raised my eyebrows in surprise, for I knew the detective had a neatly wrapped parcel in his case containing a stunning brooch from one of London's finest jewellers. And I had assumed the cake would be home-made.

"Why, flowers, my dear fellow. As proper gentlemen, we cannot arrive without them," he read my mind, replying before I could put my thoughts into words.

We stepped out in front of the station building, where a book peddler and aged florist were vying for the attention of the arriving passengers. The florist's offerings appealed to neither of us, as the blooms were wilted, surely at least a day old. It would not have surprised me had they been stolen from the nearby graveyard.

Besides the hawkers and the passengers, the only other person in the area, which expanded into a square, was the local constable with reddish whiskers. At first glance, judging by his military bearing, I guessed him to be a war veteran. He peered suspiciously at every stranger passing by and encroaching on his territory, meanwhile greeting the locals by briefly tapping two fingers to his tall helmet.

Under his hawkish gaze, we strolled into the town and headed down one of its narrow streets in the hopes of finding a nicer flower shop.

The constable continued to observe us for a moment, and then started on his rounds, pacing slowly…

***

We ascended a gentle slope along a paved alleyway and walked down the high street. There were few passers-by as lunchtime approached. Housewives were busy with preparations and their husbands were at work during the morning hours. The streets would become livelier again in the afternoon and evening, when the local elite emerged for their obligatory stroll. Gentlemen would tip their hats and ladies, behind a façade of cordiality, would observe each other with sneering expressions, seeking reasons for a later bit of gossip.

Our eyes fell on a small, charming flower shop with a painted signboard proclaiming that we were at "Rosie's." Displayed on the pavement in front of the store, beckoning to customers, were fresh tulips about to bloom, their cupped buds – protected from the sun by a canvas awning – lilting in the mild breeze.

I inhaled their scent with delight, admiring the bright colours, and followed Holmes inside, where our presence was announced by the subtle tinkle of a bell above the door. The detective looked around curiously with a murmur of satisfaction. The shop was permeated by a heady mix of floral scents, which assaulted our senses with full force. In the midst of the plethora of fresh flowers stood a sales counter with a few strips of straw for tying bouquets and a pair of garden shears. It was tidy and cosy, but neither Rosie nor anybody else was present to attend to us.

"Is there anyone here?" Holmes called out, taking a few steps towards the rear door of the shop, which led through the house and apparently on into the garden.

When there was no reply, the detective tried again while I started browsing the selection. Mrs. Hudson preferred potted plants to cut flowers, and I was had already started picking out pansy bushes with my eyes.

Finally, there was a rustle at the back and a door slammed, followed by several footsteps, and a petite young lady with her brown hair pulled back trotted into the shop. She was attired in athletic dark trousers with an apron and was carrying a bunch of fresh, bright yellow daffodils.

"My goodness, you gave me a fright," she explained on seeing us. "I hadn't heard you come in. I was working in the greenhouse and the door must have closed on me. Not many customers come in at this hour," she apologised.

She laid the daffodils on the counter and started shortening the stems with scissors to put them in a vase.

"What can I do for you, gentlemen?" she asked sweetly while working.

"We need a bouquet for a certain lady," said I, returning her smile. Given Holmes's disdain for social niceties, I took over the initiative. It was far from unpleasant, as she appeared to be a very nice young woman – had I not been her father's age, I may not have resisted the temptation to flirt.

"Then you are in the right place," she chirped. "You need only ask. Is it for a special occasion? We can also choose the flowers based on the lady's age…"

As she prattled away, she divided the cut daffodils into two bunches, adding each to a vase with other flowers that best matched in colour.

Holmes, leaning casually against one of the wooden columns in the room, gazed at the girl with animated interest, and examined her from head to food. He did so very inconspicuously, without her noticing, but knowing him as intimately as I did, I perceived the change in his manner at once.

"A shop like this must be require quite an effort," he interjected. "But I have to say you must be proud of it. Your flowers are truly first-class."

"Why, thank you, sir," she blushed. "My shop means the world to me, I do my best."

"Perhaps you could help me with something," he mused. "You see, no matter what I do, the sunflowers from my garden never last long in a vase. While yours," he pointed to one of the vases in the shop window, "are still beautiful. Might you have any advice?"

"They are sunflowers, sir. You need only place them in the sunlight, and keep them well watered, of course," she chimed laughingly, pleased with the praise.

I myself had never noticed the sunflowers in our drawing room to be suffering – indeed, I had never noticed any there at all, so I preferred to smile politely and waited to see what would come of Holmes's little charade.

Several moments of profound silence followed.

"How interesting," my friend then replied, now visibly fixing his sharp gaze upon the girl.

She in turn became quite nervous suddenly, and made it apparent she was in a hurry.

"Well then, have you chosen a flower? I wouldn't like to press you, but it is almost time for my lunch break," she cleared her throat meaningfully and took several steps towards the door.

"I am afraid there will be no deal," Holmes shook his head slowly and folded his arms.

"Then I shall thank you, and you may see yourselves out," she retorted, her demeanour likewise altered.

I hadn't the faintest idea what was going on, and why the mood in the room had cooled so suddenly. Had the girl said something to anger my friend? Why were they observing each other with such hostility?

"Do let us stop this charade," Holmes snorted in disgust, grasping the girl by the wrist.

She struggled to wriggle free and for a moment it looked like she might bite him.

"Let me go! How dare you? By what right? I will call for the police," she fumed, as a nasty grimace crept into her lovely countenance.

I was unsure whose help to come to, and was still searching for the cause of their behaviour.

"That is a brilliant idea, miss," Holmes concurred, and without troubling to explain a thing, he turned to me with icy calmness. "Watson, please be so kind as to fetch the constable. The whiskered officer who was observing us at the train station started off to the north-east, and judging by his gait, I expect you should run into him if you walk two blocks to the left from here and then turn right."

Before I could obey, a tall man with a leather sack hurtled in from the back room. He wore a knitted black cap pulled down over his eyes, for which he had cut out round holes. His eyes were malicious. I feared he might attack us, but he was clearly attempting to make an escape instead.

"Harry, you scoundrel, you're not going to leave me here?" the salesgirl hissed.

Harry the scoundrel ignored her and scrambled for the door to the street.

Holmes, without releasing his grip on the squirming wildcat, merely extended one leg to the side and knocked over an iron rod, used to pull down the awning, directly into the fugitive's path. The long pole became entangled in the man's legs, and the inertia of his forward dash threw him straight into the wall, and entirely out of action without our further assistance.

The detective rarely resorted to violence, but in this case, physics had done the job.

At that very moment, the street door flew open.

"What the devil is going on here?" thundered the constable, whom I was supposed to have sought out.

His astonished eyes darted from the concussed burglar to me, then to Holmes and the salesgirl.

Taking advantage of the girl's stunned stillness, the detective reached into her apron pocket. "Excellent! You have spared Doctor Watson the journey," he said, pleased. "If you pass through to the greenhouse in the rear, you will find the owner of this shop bound up there. In the sack on the floor, you will also find the money belonging to the poor woman, whom this fine pair of burglars have ambushed. That is, unless this young lady wishes to keep claiming that she is Rosie. She might even explain what this particular piece of headgear is for," he said, pulling a small black hood from her apron, similar to the one on the man's head.

Triumphantly, he released the girl from his iron grip, for she had nowhere to run.

"That most certainly isn't our Rosie O'Hara," the officer scowled at the now subdued woman, readying his handcuffs. "I know everyone in my district."

It all came to pass just as Holmes had predicted. The police released the bound up Rosie, who had suffered nothing but a gruesome shock, and all the money was restored to her. In return, the grateful florist rewarded us with a truly luxurious bouquet for Mrs. Hudson. By now, the reader will surely have gathered that Holmes had, with luck, broken up that dangerous pair of robbers who, according to the tabloids, had been the terror of the entire neighbourhood.

We remained on the scene for a few minutes more until the constable's reinforcements arrived.

"The only thing that eludes me is how you happened to be in the right place at the right time," Holmes inquired of the officer.

"I saw you alight from the train, and there was something familiar about you," the good man admitted.

Holmes smiled condescendingly. He often feigned disinterest in worldly fame, even declaring that his reputation as the world's greatest detective annoyed him, but I suspect it was a mere act.

"Indeed, it is I," he said, drawing a card from his breast pocket with his name embossed on it in glossy script.

"Sherlock Holmes," he introduced himself.

The constable gazed at him in astonishment. "I beg your pardon, sir, but I was not speaking of you," he said, turning to me. "It was your colleague who looked familiar. Are you not Doctor Watson? John Watson, who saved my life in Kandahar?"

I had indeed once served as an assistant surgeon with the Fifth Northumberland Rifles, but so many wounded soldiers had passed under my hands that I could hardly remember them all. The local constable must have been one of them.

It was only later that Holmes explained precisely what had occurred at the flower shop.

"It was obvious to me practically from the moment she walked in that the young woman could not have been the true shop owner," he recounted, sniffing at a tulip bud he'd plucked from the pavement and inserted into his lapel. "This shop belongs to a young lady who knows her trade. Yet the intruder behaved like an elephant in a china shop."

I was surprised, for I had observed nothing of the kind myself.

Naturally, Holmes noticed my confusion and took a long pull on his pipe to ignite it.

"Flowers, my dear Watson, like all living things, require a specific approach. Only an amateur could think that they need only be plucked or cut and put in a vase. Such a flower would not last long – it would swiftly wither and, so to speak, die. The real Rosie knows this, of course," he set about explaining.

I eagerly devoured his every word.

"Had you noticed the tulips near the entrance? Of course you did, I saw how keenly you were looking at them. You unconsciously rubbed your hands together, for a chill came over you. Do you know why? Because there were blocks of ice in the bucket with the flowers, for freshly cut flowers last longer if they are kept cool."

He was right, of course, as far as my feelings were concerned.

The detective blew out a puff of smoke indulgently and continued. "It was this detail that persuaded me to visit this particular flower shop. I was certain we would procure a much finer bouquet here than those offered by the poor woman at the train station. Every vase in the room suggested that the proprietor knew what she was doing," he motioned around the room with a sweeping gesture.

"Take these roses. See how much water they have?" he pointed to the counter. "Almost to the brim. This is because rose stems are woody and need more of it. Unlike, say, gerberas, which must be given very little water," he added, looking around. "Just as I thought, Rosie did not disappoint," he rejoiced, holding up a vase with a bright medley of ornamental yellow, red, orange and pink star-shaped blossoms. Indeed, only a few inches of water were reflected at the bottom of the vessel.

"I'm afraid I still don't understand what gave the thief away, I pondered, unsure where he was headed. "All this had been set up well before our arrival."

"The thief failed in every aspect I observed," he shrugged. "Even if I were to attribute a single thing to chance or the girl's absent-mindedness, the rest simply could not be explained otherwise than that we were face to face with a fraudster."

"Holmes, don't keep me in suspense any longer," I cried impatiently.

As usual, Holmes was enjoying the volubility with which he explained his thought processes to me as an obtuse simpleton.

"Why, it's elementary, my dear Watson! You live in nature's bosom, yet you have still learned nothing from our gardener?" he laughed drily. "First off, I was struck by the daffodils. She must have picked them up hastily as a prop when she hurried into the shop to stop us from proceeding into the back rooms. For Rosie was lying there bound up and guarded by the thief's accomplice, Harry, and it was of the essence that we not see them."

"What was so special about the daffodils?"

"Nothing about the daffodils as such. But the imposter put them in a vase with other flowers without a moment's hesitation. No proper florist would do that. Every expert knows that the stems of daffodils produce a fluid, a kind of sap, which is harmful to other plants."

"Meaning they must be displayed separately," I understood.

"Yes, at least for the first few hours after being cut, until the sap leaks out."

"So the sunflowers were just a test?"

"Quite so, to make her betray herself entirely by advising me to put them in the sun and give them water. An experienced florist would know that sunflowers must be immersed in boiling water for five to seven seconds, to expand the veins, allowing the plant to absorb more water."

"Where in Heaven's name do you get this knowledge?"

"Merely by observing the world around us, my dear fellow. Incidentally, you may have noticed something suspicious yourself, despite your ignorance of floriculture."

"What do you mean?"

"It might have struck you as odd that, although the woman claimed we had disturbed her while working in the greenhouse, she had no soil on her hands. Even more so, that her nails were clean and lacquered, and her skin entirely unblemished. Nobody who is constantly in contact with thorns, vines and twigs has hands like that."

As always, it all seemed so simple once Holmes had explained it.

We bade the constable and Rosie a cordial farewell and took a cab to the Hudsons, who had surely been awaiting us eagerly. The incident was promptly forgotten, for in our lives full of criminal masterminds, cunning swindlers and deceitful murderers, it was a mere morning's trifle.

For the rest of the journey, over the rattling carriage wheels, Holmes engaged in something else – a lecture on why a fly, because of its compound eyes, perceives space differently, and is thus often unable to find its way out of the open window through which it has entered. He only fell silent at lunch, when an exquisite trout was served.

THE DISAPPEARANCE

OF THE WIDOW HAMISHAM

Among our favourite pastimes, which Holmes and I regularly indulged in for years, were long walks about the city. We particularly enjoyed strolling through one neighbourhood, which was full of old villas, ancient houses and spacious parks, often frequented by Londoners on foot or on horseback. There was one place in particular that had been arousing our curiosity for some time – a dilapidated townhouse, which stuck out from the otherwise well-kept development like a rotten tooth in a bright smile. Yet we had never been inside and for many years knew not to whom it belonged.

We found out only when the building became the focus of our interest at the beginning of another case. Allegedly, only one old lady lived in the large house, and quite modestly at that, given how wealthy she was. She practically occupied only the bedroom and drawing room on the ground floor, in the company of two cats. She never ventured out and almost nobody visited her. Therefore, her sudden disappearance went unnoticed for several days.

The only person who took note of Mrs. Hamisham's absence was her housemaid, Miss Lucy Forrester, insistent on using this title despite being almost as old as her employer, who was supposed to be about eighty.

In her own words, Miss Forrester visited Margaret Hamisham once a week, every Wednesday, to attend to various household chores and deliver groceries for the week to come. This unvarying ritual had been going on with strict regularity for countless years – until today, when Miss Forrester failed to find the old lady at home, with no prior word of warning.

It was this fact, which she could not explain otherwise than by imagining the darkest scenarios, which so disturbed Miss Forrester that she determined to visit my friend.

Sherlock Holmes had her explain everything in thorough detail, and needed no further encouragement. We set off for the given address immediately, but because it was a busy weekday morning, the cab ploughed through the heavy traffic at a sluggish pace. The detective employed this time by posing additional questions.

"Does Mrs. Hamisham suffer from any illnesses, which might have caused her to be hospitalised?"

"She has some heart problems and emphysema, so she mustn't be upset or exert herself," Miss Forrester lamented. "It was the first thing I thought of. But she hadn't sent for her physician, and she is not at any of the nearby hospitals I checked with. I spent the entire morning doing the rounds! She has disappeared into thin air!"

"Are you sure the lady is not indoors somewhere? It is a rambling house…"

"Mr. Holmes, the house is indeed a labyrinth, but I searched everywhere I could, believe me. Moreover, the lady cannot get up the steps without assistance, which is why she never goes upstairs anymore."

"Hence you believe it equally impossible that she would have gone outside," I clarified.

"Oh yes, Doctor Watson. Entirely out of the question. Mrs. Margaret only ever goes out in the back garden on occasion, and only when the sun isn't shining. She doesn't like the sun, considers it unhealthy, and finds tanned skin repugnant."

Had I heard this argument under different circumstances, I would have felt the desire to smirk, for I still encountered, from time to time, old-fashioned opinions regarding the Elizabethan ideal of beauty, which embraced an ivory complexion. It has long since been medically proven that the sun does no harm to the skin, and is, on the contrary, beneficial.

Some minutes later, our cab stopped moving entirely. The street ahead had been blocked by a produce farmer, and our driver was scolding him vocally.

We had barely reached the end of Baker Street near the underground station, which had been gaining popularity in central London. Stations along the metropolitan railway, originally connecting the railway stations at Paddington and Farringdon*, were popping up like mushrooms, for they greatly accelerated travel across the city, especially on days like this one. Although I am no opponent of progress, Holmes and I used it seldom, indeed hardly at all. The surface tunnels were full of smoke and steam from the locomotives, which made me feel unwell, not to mention the odour that penetrated all our clothing. It was enough that I had to tolerate the exotic tobacco fumes from Holmes's pipes all my life.

Mrs. Hamisham's mysterious disappearance may have persuaded us to expedite our journey in this manner, but unfortunately, the "tube," as the locals called this mode of transportation, did not yet run to the neighbourhood where she resided. We thus had to endure the lengthy journey by cab, during which Miss Forrester became increasingly panic-stricken.

At last we stood before the stately building with a miniature front garden and shabby, dark brown façade. It looked abandoned, unkempt, and we now understood why. The old lady lacked the energy and strength, and quite possibly even interest in what her home looked like from the outside.

A gate in a low wall covered with moss and lichen led to the black lacquered main door. Miss Forrester unlocked it and stepped inside first, whereupon she gave a startled yelp and jumped back, almost knocking me and Holmes over!

I caught her in my arms and my friend swiftly stepped round her to see what had frightened her.

A white cat was feasting on a disembowelled mouse on a rug in the entrance hall. It now measured a cool stare in our direction, then hissed, snatched up its prey and ran off, leaving behind only a few long hairs and several drops of blood on the oriental doormat.

"It's just a cat, performing its primary duty as a pest hunter," Holmes observed.

"If you please, sir, that isn't normal," Miss Forrester objected, shuddering. "Mrs. Hamisham's cats, Mindy and Wendy, are… how shall I put this… the only creatures she likes. She spoils them rotten. She buys them liver from the butcher's shop, which I mince up, to keep their coats shiny. With all due respect, those Persians are better fed than my husband and children. If they've started hunting mice, they must be hungry because nobody has fed them for several days."

The detective gazed thoughtfully into the dark corner where the animal had disappeared.

"Let us begin our search. Only once I am satisfied that the house is indeed empty shall we consider our next course of action," Holmes decided, and asked the housemaid to show him around.

One could go in several directions from the hall. To the right of the main door was the entrance to the dining room and kitchen, while the drawing room was on the left, leading back to another room, which was presently converted into the landlady's bedroom. Directly across from the entrance rose a broad staircase ending in a landing with a ficus plant and a large mirror in a massive frame. Here, the staircase split into two arms leading to the upper floor. Beneath the stairs, set in the wood panelling, was an almost invisible door leading to the cellar. At the end of the hall was a doorway opening onto a grass-covered yard.

Holmes's examination of the ground floor was fairly swift, but nonetheless typically thorough. Yet neither he nor I noticed anything that would indicate when, how and in what condition Margaret Hamisham had disappeared.

The place was clean and tidy, devoid of any suspicious articles or clothing strewn about in haste. Quite unlike the exterior, the inside of the house looked considerably better. The mahogany furniture in the drawing room smelled of fresh polish, the upholstery on the chairs and sofas was well kept, and the china in the display case gleamed spotlessly. An oriental smoking set took pride of place. Holmes, himself an avid smoker, gave it a mere fleeting glance and moved on indifferently.

The iron-framed bed with its headboard in the back room were simply made, and on the nightstand with a petroleum lamp lay a volume of Jane Austen with a leather bookmark. On the wool bedspread was a depression left by the cats, who had evidently not given up their habit of sleeping on the bed, even without their owner to keep them warm.

After a thorough inspection of the kitchen, with a cast iron stove and heavy oak table, a well-stocked pantry and other rooms, we descended to the cellar, which was filled with clutter. We searched every place where the helpless old lady might have fallen, or where she may have accidentally injured herself, but to no avail. The only thing we found was the soiled cat litter, which those fastidious animals were still using.

We returned to the drawing room, no wiser than we had been.

"Does madam have any kin?" Holmes asked, searching in vain for family photographs. There was but one faded image of a handsome man with a trimmed beard, holding a cigar and posing in a light tropical suit, poised on the shelf.

"No, not that I know of," Miss Forrester shook her head helplessly. "She had no children and her husband passed more than forty years ago. When she had a mind, which was not especially often, she recounted how they had travelled the world together. As far as I know, he worked in the civil service, the foreign ministry maybe. I always thought she must have been very happy with him. She only became embittered in the course of a long, lonely life."

"So there are no siblings, nephews, nieces?"

"No, I'm sure she has nobody."

"You said she has no visitors either. Why did she, or rather does she, live in such solitude?" I wondered, ashamed of my mistake in having spoken of the lady as already dead.

"I don't believe she ever felt lonely," the housekeeper sighed. "But it must be said that madam is a very particular person. She loves the old ways, is reserved, does not make friends or seek out company. The world outside her door only bothers her. She dislikes change and considers the modern age perverse and degenerate. She is quite satisfied enclosed in her shell behind the walls of this house."

"How wealthy is she?" the detective pursued his questioning.

"Oh, she never confided her financial affairs to me. But if you look around, this house alone and everything in it suggests a considerable fortune!"

"Does she wear any jewellery?"

"Who for?" exclaimed the lady. "No, the madam lives quite plainly, she does not indulge in ostentation. Why, she even refused when my husband and I once offered to buy her a gramophone."

"Do you know if she made a will?"

"All of Mrs. Hamisham's documents are in the custody of Mr. Reynolds. His office is at Charing Cross Road. If there is a will, it must be with him."

Looking around, the detective stopped at the window and looked out through the curtains. "Is there anything missing? When you were searching the house for the lady, did you notice anything suspicious?" he asked, pressing for more clues. We had precious few so far.

"I haven't noticed anything missing."

"How does she pay your wage?"

"Once a month, in cash."

"Do you know where she hides the money?"

Miss Forrester nodded. "Every few months, madam sends me to the bank with a cheque to cash. She then uses the money to pay for running the household. She keeps it in a small black purse, which she always keeps close at hand. It also contains her medicine, which I prepare for her for the coming week, and some other little items."

Yet we had not found any such purse.

"So there is something missing, after all. Summing it all up, the fact are as follows," Holmes mused. "Mrs. Hamisham disappeared sometime after your visit last Wednesday, some three to five days ago, considering the hungry cats. Had she undertaken to do so on her own, it would be contrary to all her habits and essentially beyond her physical abilities, as you claim. Whatever it was that induced her to leave her house, it was unexpected, and she must have had assistance from someone. Someone who did not forget about her indispensable purse. Hence, he or she must have been aware of her condition – and there are not many such people."

It took the housekeeper a moment before she realised why the detective had fixed a meaningful look upon her.

"I say!" she exclaimed indignantly. "You cannot possibly assume that I…?"

"I never assume anything," my friend shrugged, adding "I merely deduce from the available information. If a crime has indeed occurred here – and I am not yet entirely convinced that any did, for there is no victim or motive – the culprit must be somebody close. And in this case, there are few such people."

"She may have been randomly assaulted or burgled. A desperate and hungry vagrant, a thief acting on impulse," I objected. "Such incidents do happen."

"Then the scene would be quite different, and more than just one purse would be missing," Holmes disagreed. "No, this does not fit a burglary."

"Well then, what shall we do?"

"I'm afraid we have nothing to go upon, so there is very little we can do," said the detective, turning towards Miss Forrester, who was still fuming. "Miss, I have two suggestions for you. First off, please feed the cats. Then, contact the nearest constabulary and report the disappearance. The Yard is far better equipped to put out a missing person's alert than I am with my network of little street urchins**," he added.

She muttered that she had expected rather more from Holmes than to be sent to the police, but she obeyed. Before she left, we agreed to conduct another search of the upper floors of the house, and then shut the door behind us. We would keep the housekeeper informed, should we or the police discover anything new.

"Do we really not know how to proceed?" I asked incredulously as the door closed behind her.

"What a naïve question, Watson!" Holmes chided me amiably. "Of course we do. But we needn't have Miss Forrester breathing down our necks to do it. I do not actually suspect her, but she has already told us everything she possibly can."

He bid me follow him up the stairs, where we peered into the various rooms. The housekeeper was not exaggerating when she termed the house labyrinthine. For somebody visiting it for the first time, the layout of the rooms was remarkably confusing, the positioning of the doors and other passageways showed little logic, and I would easily have become lost were it not for Holmes and his keen sense of orientation.

Nor was our search eased by the fact that the house was literally crammed with objects of every imaginable kind.

Although Mrs. Margaret occupied the lower floor with minimal furnishings, the upstairs was overflowing with curios and collections, apparently accumulated with her beloved husband on their travels. There were articles from the Far East, Asia and America – even the head of a rare white bison trophy hanging on one wall.

I cannot imagine a single museum that would refuse such a collection.

"It is odd that she collects so many things, yet is unable to enjoy them," I remarked.

Had time not been of the essence, Holmes would doubtless have liked to immerse himself in the clutter and examine every curio and rarity one piece at a time. "They are of profound emotional value to her. She is unable to part with them, and just knowing she has them is enough," he surmised. I believe he understood her feelings.

A library full of rare volumes also occupied two rooms, where I spotted a number of unique first editions of classics. Many of the shelves, cabinets, commodes and other furniture were covered with linen sheets to protect them from dust. The crystal chandeliers and historical armour were likewise draped with greyish covers. It all made me feel as though I were in a haunted house, just waiting for something to move.

The faint musty odour only intensified this atmosphere.

"I wouldn't be surprised if somebody had concealed the old lady's body under one of those sheets," I remarked, with a chill running down my spine. "A thorough search of this entire place would be a job for days, even for several people."

"It would be exceedingly melodramatic to wrap her in sheets and hide her here," Holmes frowned, returning to the corridor leading to the staircase, where he crouched down to examine something on the floor. "Aha, just as I thought," he added after a moment, and fell silent again.

"You may think I am a mind-reader Holmes, but I must disabuse you of that error," I said, clearing my throat after he had been silent too long. "Have you found something?"

"Forgive me, my dear fellow. I got lost in my musings," he apologised, rising again. "I have found nothing, except the dust stirred up by our footsteps. Which indicates the following – Miss Forrester has long since relaxed in cleaning the upper floors, or rather, given up on it altogether. Why should she bother, if the old lady never comes up? She hasn't swept here for months," he declared with satisfaction.

"But we are not dealing with the case of a lazy housekeeper," I pointed out.

"Quite so, my friend," he smiled. "Nevertheless, it has provided a valuable clue to our investigation. Had somebody dragged the body and hidden it anywhere up here, they would have left traces. Dust wiped off here and there, a torn cobweb. No, nothing has been moved here for ages."

"So if Margaret Hamisham truly isn't in the house, then surely you did the right thing by having it reported," I judged. "And we have but to wait."

But Holmes corrected me.

"I believe the answer lies somewhere in this house. But we must search for it outside!"

***

Sherlock Holmes never did anything gratuitously. If he looked out a window while examining a room, it was only to determine which of the windows opposite offered a reciprocal view.

Hence, we headed forthwith to the doors of the more affordable tenements opposite, separated from the finer homes by a street and small park. We did so immediately upon leaving Mrs. Havisham's house and closing the gate behind us. My friend had picked out two entrances, and one of them proved most successful, with a nosy and talkative neighbour, a middle-aged housewife, who spent most of her time observing her surroundings. Where would crime investigation be without these good souls?

In the torrent of words unleashed upon us, which I am unable to reproduce here with any accuracy, there was one crucial piece of information. For it was not entirely true that nobody ever visited the old lady. In recent months and weeks, several gentlemen had allegedly appeared at her door, the latest even arriving after dark.

"How are we to understand this? Are you questioning the lady's honour?" I asked, horrified. "Why, she is infirm and elderly!"

"You asked me if I'd seen anybody, so I'm answering," the neighbour retorted. "It was somebody different each time, and he always arrived in a carriage."

"How long have you been observing these visits?" Holmes inquired.

"I can't say exactly. It all started some time ago," she shrugged. "First it was once in a while, then they visited more and more often. You know what was interesting? The first ones came in ordinary cabs, and later the gentlemen became ever finer looking, always arriving in fancier carriages."

"When was the last time you saw somebody here?"

"Was Thursday, I think, just this past Thursday," she recalled.

So the lady had still been at home on Thursday? Once again, we had something to think about. The neighbour had seen nothing else, claiming she didn't have time to snoop at the weekends, when her husband was home. In any case, the information meant some progress.

Holmes wanted to pay one more visit that day, to Mr. Reynolds.

The solicitor, who had many prominent clients, was somewhat startled when we stopped by his office at the address mentioned by Miss Forrester. However, upon hearing my friend's name and receiving his assurances that he was acting in the best interests of his client, and that the matter could be quite a grave one, he conceded to cooperate.

"You will surely understand that I cannot violate certain principles connected with my office," he said as he received us and showed us to a pair of comfortable leather armchairs.

"We need only speak on a general level," Holmes assured him, and proceeded to describe the affair. "Naturally, it is still possible that Mrs. Hamisham will appear, alive and well, with a logical explanation. Nevertheless, it is my aim to prevent any potential impending danger she may be facing, in the hope that it is not yet too late. And we know of no other acquaintance of hers, apart from you."

Reynolds nodded grimly. "I shall do my utmost to help."

"Do you have her will in your custody?" the detective inquired, leaning towards him with urgency. "In other words – is there anybody who would benefit from her possible demise?"

"Mrs. Hamisham's will is sealed in my office," the solicitor confirmed, but promptly dissipated our hopes of perhaps identifying a motive. "Upon her death, Mrs. Hamisham's assets will be divided among severable charitable organisations and animal welfare societies."

Alas, no particular suspect, I thought fleetingly.

Reynolds made matters even worse. "Moreover, none of the societies know anything about it. They will only be informed once the sad event comes to pass."

Holmes pressed his elbows into the armrest, steepling his hands under his chin thoughtfully.

"What shall become of the house?"

"The same as the remaining property. It will be sold at auction and the proceeds will be included in the bequest.

Speaking of which, I can tell you one more thing," the solicitor confided. "Madam sent me a telegram requesting a private consultation at her home. However, she did not inform me beforehand what the issue was."

My attention peaked, and even Holmes raised his eyebrows. "When did you receive this telegram?"

"On Friday."

"May I see it?" the detective asked.

"I'm afraid I did not keep it," Reynold apologised. "I merely checked the next possible date and time, sent a reply and threw the telegram away."

My friend sighed with frustration. "There is nothing to be done. When was your appointment to be?"

"The morning after tomorrow. It was supposedly an important matter, but not downright urgent."

We rose to depart. "Just to be certain – is there nothing among her documents that could indicate what the issue could have been?" Holmes tried once more.

"As somebody who is accustomed to reading between the lines, I can assure you there was nothing that could render Mrs. Hamisham the target of a premeditated crime. All her affairs are in order, she has no debts, her house is not encumbered by a mortgage – there is nothing at all."

So we parted, unreconciled. More questions had been raised than answered.

We hailed a cab to return home and found ourselves again immersed in the chaos of the bustling city. The traffic in the afternoon was so dense that sandwich sellers and newspaper vendors passed among the carriages, buggies and carts, hawking their goods to the bored passengers. Even we were unable to hold out until dinner, served by Mrs. Hudson, and bought some fragrant fish and chips in a greasy newspaper for the journey.

"Who do you think those gentlemen visiting Mrs. Hamisham could have been?" I asked. "And what could she have wanted to discuss with her solicitor?"

"I regret I haven't the faintest idea, so far," the detective said, pecking absently at his meal. "In any case, the matter is taking on decidedly interesting contours."

"How can it be that Miss Forrester knew nothing about it?"

"We know the old lady was not especially forthcoming. It was nothing she needed to share with her housekeeper," he replied.

I left him to ponder the matter without further interruption, but could not help feeling that we were too late to avert a crime. Knowing my friend, he was thinking the same thing.

***

Holmes measured the complexity of a problem by the number of pipes he smoked while solving it. Usually, a case required two to three pipes, but this time he spent the entire evening and night next to the hearth in our drawing room, and by morning not a leaf was left in the tobacco pouch. He was tired, exhausted, but the disappearance of the widow Hamisham would not let him sleep.

Regrettably, the worst possible denouement came before breakfast with the arrival of Inspector Lestrade, just when I had finally manged to persuade the detective to get some rest.

For our good old acquaintance, Scotland Yard investigator Lestrade, in equal parts ambitious, eager, hasty and rash, had come to inform us that Mrs. Hamisham had been found.

Dead, in her house.

"Impossible!" my friend exclaimed, jumping from the armchair in which he had heard the news.

"Do not be upset, Mr. Holmes, and do let me finish," the inspector calmed him. "Indeed, she was not at home yesterday evening. She only returned late at night, in a carriage. The neighbour you'd seen and questioned yesterday reported it to the local police officer this morning. He went to check on Mrs. Hamisham, got into the house and found her. Because I was aware from Miss Forrester's report that you had initiated a search for the missing lady, I wanted to inform you about it."

"How did she die?" the detective asked, exasperated.

"Heart failure," the inspector replied. "Natural causes."

Holmes snorted angrily. "I want to see her. Watson, be so kind as to get ready," he bid to me, piercing Lestrade with his eyes.

"I do hope you don't mind?"

The inspector's face betrayed suppressed annoyance, but he didn't dare object. In his mind, however, he was doubtless regretting the professional courtesy that had brought him to us.

A carriage was waiting for Lestrade outside, and as it was still fairly early in the morning, we managed the avoid the rush hour this time. We stopped in front of Mrs. Hamisham's house in a fraction of the time the journey had required just the day before. Holmes's fatigue was gone, and his brain was working at full tilt.

A doctor's buggy and a hearse with the undertakers in black top hats were standing by the curb. We noticed the chatty neighbour from across the street in the crowd of onlookers.

Holmes strode up to her first.

"Please be so kind, madam," he greeted her, "and tell us precisely what it is you saw last night? I know you've already told my colleagues, but I suspect they cannot hear for words," he said, taking a bitter dig at the police officers.

"Well now, it was dark, and it was across the street," she began hesitantly. "The rattle of wheels woke me. A covered coach stopped out front, and the lady alighted and ran into the house. The coachman and outrider took a trunk down from the rack, carried it inside and then left."

"How long were they inside?"

"About half an hour."

"Rather a long time, wouldn't you think?" the detective said, looking pointedly at Lestrade.

"They were helping an old lady," the inspector reminded him. "Perhaps they were dragging the trunk upstairs, for all I know."

"Perhaps. And perhaps you will be promoted prematurely," the detective retorted snidely, and strode off into the house. I followed him swiftly, and we took no further interest in the offended Lestrade.

Mrs. Hamisham was stretched on her bed, a small, frail old woman with snowy white hair and a stern, thin face that betrayed her pertinacity and obstinacy. She lay on her back, hands folded over her breast, as though she had only just fallen asleep.

Next to her on the nightstand was a purse full of money and a tube of medicine.

The police physician in attendance repeated the cause of death, which we had already learned from Lestrade, but Holmes asked me to conduct my own assessment.

I examined the body carefully, but until an autopsy was carried out, my options were limited. Hence, in concurrence with the police report, I had to state there were no apparent signs of violence on the body of the deceased, her oral cavity was clean, there was nothing to suggest the ingestion of poison orally or its injection, and given her known diagnosis and ailing heart, it could indeed have been a heart attack. Rigor mortis was already becoming apparent on the body.

"So you see, even Doctor Watson is on our side," boasted Lestrade.

"Do not distort my words," I chided him, feeling like a traitor.

Holmes was evidently surprised.

"Perhaps," he said, ignoring us and thinking frantically aloud. "Perhaps it all happened differently."

"Or perhaps you are simply wrong this time, and are seeking a sensation where there is none," the inspector returned caustically.

There was a metal tin with butter biscuits marked Greetings from Torquay on the table, which had not been there before. The policeman pointed to it as irrefutable evidence. "She simply departed for the weekend to get some sun, and returned last night. Unfortunately, the journey left her exhausted and the lady succumbed to cardiac arrest. Is that so hard to believe? Just because she hadn't told her housekeeper about the planned trip? It is obvious, judging by her purse, that it was hardly a case of theft."

It was also true that she had returned in time for her appointment with Reynolds, which would be consistent with a recreational outing, as I took the liberty of pointing out to Holmes.

He made no reply, his eyes darting about the room.

He stopped abruptly near the display cabinet. There was a gaping empty space where the oriental smoking set had been only yesterday.

His eyebrows shot up and he started searching for the set excitedly, but even after telling the surprised inspector what he was looking for, Lestrade retained his usual scepticism.

"Something of the sort can hardly be considered a motive for a cardinal crime," he yawned, unconvinced.

Nor could I think of any explanation, other than that the owner may have put it somewhere herself.

"Can you not see that everything about it is wrong?" Holmes said despairingly. "Lestrade's lazy and convenient deductions come as no surprise, but you, Watson…?"

He suddenly became alert, listening attentively.

"Do you hear that?" he asked.

"What? I can't hear a thing," Lestrade raised his head, eyes twitching from side to side.

Holmes led us towards the sound, which only he could hear at this point. He returned to the hallway and opened the door to the back yard. Two large cats, unaccustomed to spending the night outdoors, leapt inside with shrill meows. Someone must have chased them out.

"Mrs. Hamisham's cats," I explained to the inspector.

"Well aren't you an adorable little puss," he said, leaning over one of them, but it returned the favour with a slash of its claws.

"They are spoiled and dislike strangers," I added, as Lestrade jumped back with a curse.

The detective perused the empty courtyard. "Somebody was here last night," he deduced. "There are fresh footprints in the grass, and scratches on the rear gate where somebody picked the lock with a skeleton key. Is this still not enough, Inspector?"

Lestrade was no genius, but he was no fool either. When he saw Holmes's dogged insistence, he tried at the least to understand.

"Very well then, what is your version of the events?" he asked, folding his arms condescendingly over his chest.

My friend, on the other hand, knew that without evidence, he could not offer up an incomplete theory, which the police officer would tear to shreds.

"I shall give you an answer by this evening, if you agree?" he proposed to the inspector. "If you do not hear from me by then, you may close the case as a death without foul play, and publicly declare that I was mistaken."

Those were high stakes indeed.

Our professional adversary's eyes glittered in his pointy face upon hearing the proposition.

***

When the body had been taken away and the inspector and his men had disappeared, Holmes and I remained alone in the house. We stood on the threshold of one of the rooms with Mrs. Hamisham's collection of souvenirs, her cats meandering about our legs. They seemed to sense that were it not for us, they would not be fed and would most likely spend the night outdoors. Their white hairs clung to my trousers.

"I am starting to perceive the outlines of what happened, but several crucial pieces to the puzzle are still missing," the detective admitted. "I suspect what occurred, and how, but that is all."

The essential fact was that there was no suspect.

"You are still better off than I or Lestrade," I replied.

My friend gave me an almost pitying glance. "Tonight's events are quite obvious," he began to fill me in on what was already a certainty in his mind. "The lady did not return home alive."

"How can you be so sure?"

"Because of the heart pills that remained in her purse. Miss Forrester counted them out for her mistress beforehand, and had the latter died last night, there would have been none left. Yet several remained in the tube. Why had she stopped taking them?"

"Because she was dead…" admitted I.

89

He grunted in agreement. "She died one or two days earlier in a place as yet unknown to me, but somebody went to considerable lengths to make it look as though she had returned. Apparently, her death came as a surprise, and he had to decide what to do. As you know, rigor mortis can be delayed if the body is kept warm. All that was needed then was for anybody with a slight figure to throw the lady's overcoat over her shoulders and imitate her gait. The other two men bore the trunk in which her body was concealed. Once in the bedroom, they arranged and staged everything, and the individual impersonating the widow left by the back door through the courtyard. The entire party knew somebody could be watching them from the neighbouring houses, hence the theatrics."

"The cats must have got out during the escape via the back door. They most likely took off as well," I suggested. "Mrs. Hamisham would not have let them go outside."

Holmes nodded approvingly.

"Thanks to Mr. Reynolds, we also know who may have gained from the lady's death."

This part still eluded me. "Why, the societies that stood to inherit know nothing about it!"

"But the inheritance is not the issue," the detective said to my surprise. "Not in the true sense of the word. However, we did learn that the entire estate is to be auctioned off, and we also know how fondly the old lady clung to her things. She did not wish to get rid of them or sell them. Yet somebody so greatly coveted one of the items in her collection that they finally decided, when Mrs. Hamisham refused to give it up on good terms, to find a different means."

"Could it have been the smoking set?"

"Certainly not, the inspector is not mistaken in that regard. All the same, a theory is developing in my mind as to what role that particular item may have played. But the culprit was after something else, and there is nothing standing in his way now."

It began to dawn on me. "Now, the person responsible for her death need only await the auction in order to obtain the item in question without greater difficulty."

"Precisely," said Holmes. "The carriages that had recently been delivering visitors Mrs. Hamisham's door brought ever newer and more important emissaries from this unknown individual. The last, most luxurious of them, would seem to have brought our stranger himself. Yet to no avail, the widow refused to give in."

"And on Friday, she summoned her solicitor..." I continued, matching the pace of this thoughts.

"I would not be surprised if she had desired to open her will and make an amendment. I think she resented the duress being exerted on her, and wanted to change her will, to prevent something. She preferred to summon Reynolds immediately, rather than waiting until Wednesday to send Miss Forrester to fetch him," the detective added. "Unfortunately, she underestimated her pursuer's obstinacy. We can only guess what happened next. Perhaps the person paid one more visit at the weekend, but it is more likely that he sent yet another intermediary, who appeared to be trustworthy and somehow persuaded madam to leave with him. Another round of insistence followed, perhaps even extortion. The old lady, unable to withstand it, collapsed."

I frowned. "Why didn't they fetch a doctor? Or take her to the hospital?"

"For fear of discreditation," Holmes drew a possible conclusion. "Anybody with an expensive carriage must be wealthy, perhaps even of noble blood. He panicked – he did not want to be responsible for a strange old lady passing away in his house. How would he possibly explain it?"

"But – who was it then?"

"That is the question," Holmes groaned, pointing to the plethora of artefacts. "Each of these items could represent the holy grail for a particular collector, but there are thousands of them before our eyes. Which one cost the lady her life?"

We were faced with a task that was tantamount to the proverbial search for a needle in a haystack.

"Without the final piece of the puzzle and proof, it is but a worthless idea," the detective despaired.

My friend rarely looked utterly perplexed, but as he wandered among the shelves of collections, it was perhaps the closest I'd ever seen him come to such a condition.

Moreover, we were pressed for time. I had no doubt that Lestrade would readily make a critical mention of Holmes in the press.

The detective paused in front of one of the shelves, half covered with a dust sheet, and thrust his hands into his coat pockets. An expression of surprise came over his face as he felt for something in one of them, and pulled out the crumpled piece of newspaper from yesterday's fish and chips.

He was about to discard it, when something in the torn newsprint caught his eye. I noticed the large headline about the current urban boom and the building of infrastructure – nothing of particular interest.

In Holmes's mind, however, it seemed to have triggered an association that connected the crucial pieces of the puzzle.

"Why, of course!" he exclaimed. "I reproach Lestrade for not hearing for words, yet I myself have failed to see!"

He turned to me with sparkling eyes.

"Watson, ask me nothing. I must ascertain something first. But if I am right, it will be a sure thing," he hooted, already dragging me downstairs by my coat sleeve, taking two steps at a time. Outside he hailed the first available cab to drive us to the headquarters of the London County Council – the main administrative authority of our great city. There he left me waiting outside, returning a good half-hour later, exceedingly pleased with whatever he had discovered.

"I am ready to close the case," he announced, glancing at his pocket watch. "With a bit of luck, I will serve the solution to our friend the inspector on a silver tray, just in time for afternoon tea, giving us time to visit the opera performance you mentioned last week."

All of a sudden, he was yet again the confident and resolute Holmes, who knew all the answers.

"Who are we going to see now?"

The detective gave me the prestigious address of a respectable businessman and philanthropist.

I wondered what he could possibly have to do with our case, but whistled obediently to hail another cab. But this time, my friend declined.

"No, we shall take the underground," he decided.

I was far from thrilled, but I assumed Holmes did not want to risk another traffic jam. On our way to the nearest metropolitan station, for Heaven knows what reason, he recounted how many stops on the newly constructed "tube" were connected with haunted sites, and all the legends and superstitions that plagued them.

"Did you know, for instance, that at the station near Farringdon, passengers on the last night train hear the chilling moans of the Screaming Ghost?" he revealed. "It was just there that a certain Anne Naylor was killed in 1758."

He took an eager interest in such legends, so it came as no surprise to me that he knew so many.

"Or Aldgate station, for example, which was built at the location of the epicentre of the Great Plague of 1665. Almost a thousand victims are buried at the site," he remarked as we reached the platform and waited for our connection.

"What made you think of these tales just now?"

"Because there will soon be another station in London associated with death."

"You mean…" I faltered, taken aback.

"Yes," he said, confirming my reasoning, and gave me his arm to help me into the car that had arrived. No sooner had we taken our seats, the steam engine whistled, gathered speed and plunged from the station into a dark tunnel which, as I had feared, filled up rapidly with unpleasant smoke.

"The underground is the future of the city," Holmes continued. "It is booming incredibly fast. Countless private companies and investors have put up money for the construction of the metropolitan railway, and it is in their interest to keep building new stops. We even have a tunnel under the Thames, and the daily number of passengers is around ten thousand. Indeed, they have started building new electric cars, which will soon rid us of the unpleasant fumes. There are vast amounts of money involved."

"But… what does anything in Mrs. Hamisham's collections have to do with how the underground is built?"

We emerged in yet another station, where more passengers boarded.

"The answer is not concealed in the house. The answer is the house itself," he revealed finally.

It did not take long for me to put it all together as follows.

"The underground does not yet run to the neighbourhood where Mrs. Hamisham resided, but that is soon to change," I realised.

"Quite so," the detective confirmed, overcome once more by sadness. This time, not because of his own inability to solve the puzzle, but because somebody was so greedy that they wouldn't shy away even from terrorising a stubborn old lady.

"The house stands at a crucial location for the expansion of the railway. Plenty of demolition is required wherever something new is to be built. Hence, the owner of the investment company building the new metropolitan line had an eminent interest in purchasing the site. He needed to acquire it at any cost, for the tunnel cannot go anywhere else. Nor could he wait, as construction is to begin forthwith. It is set in stone in the city's zoning plans. When his emissaries failed to break the lady's resolve, and further visitors left her unconvinced, he lured her to his own residence, putting her under excessive duress for several days."

"How do you suppose he persuaded her to leave with him or his lackeys? By force?"

"No, he wouldn't have dared. He is, after all, a gentleman. He used bait, thanks to which she went willingly. She even took her purse, like a proper lady."

I didn't attempt to conceal that I had no idea what this ruse could have been.

"Mrs. Hamisham only cared about one thing, and that was her beloved late husband, whose belongings she still clings to," Holmes reminded me. "This is where that oriental smoking set comes into play – it did not belong to the old lady, as she could hardly have smoked with her emphysema. At first glance, it did not fit in with the things she kept upstairs, for it was almost new. You will readily find similar ones in the souvenir shops at Piccadilly Circus. I believe it was brought to her as a lure, and madam had it placed in the display cabinet immediately. Then they told her a story about it having belonged to her husband, whom they may have encountered somewhere on their travels."

"So, the old lady made a rare exception and accepted an invitation to tea or dinner, believing she had found a kindred spirit and someone to glorify her husband with," I grasped the meaning.

"She was too late in discovering the truth, whose residence she was at and why…" Holmes concluded.

I imagined how Mrs. Hamisham must have felt when she learned how she had been deceived. The final straw must have been finding out why they were so determined to buy her house. "Madam was not just sentimental, but entirely out of touch with modern times. These two factors came together into something her heart literally could not overcome. I'm not surprised it broke," I remarked.

By then we had almost reached our destination. This mode of urban transport was rapid indeed.

"But do you know what it all means?" I asked Holmes as we alighted from the car and set out for the residence of the businessman, or more precisely the chairman of The Tube Company Ltd.

"Yes, I do," the detective pursed his lips in anger. "It was not murder as such. But the manner in which they treated the lady, quite literally bringing about her death, is highly immoral. I will not allow such behaviour to go unpunished. On this occasion, I will take the liberty of exploiting your contacts in the press, whose condemnation will be a far greater blow to this individual than the hand of the law."

I could presently go into the details of the later stages of the investigation, but they are decidedly less interesting.

In brief, they are as follows:

At the unscrupulous gentleman's residence, we also met his wife, who was of the same slight stature as the poor Mrs. Hamisham and apparently played a role in the "old lady's return." They both denied any acquaintance with the madam, or that she had ever been a visitor to their home, but were incriminated in the end by the hairs of a white Persian cat in the guest room. Having no pets of their own, this evidence could only have got there on Mrs. Hamisham's dress. What's more, fresh feline scratches stood out on the forearms of the master of the house.

Once several identical tins of biscuits from Torquay, a gift from relatives, were found in the pantry, followed by a receipt for the cheap smoking set in the study, the lady broke down and confessed on behalf of both culprits, much to her husband's dismay.

They had supposedly retrieved the smoking set and disposed of it in the Thames to cover up their tracks. Paradoxically – had they left it in its place – Holmes may not have given it such attention.

The Tube Company went bankrupt and had no further part in the development of London's metropolitan railway, but this did little to slow down its expansion.

Indeed, a new tube stop was later built on the site of Mrs. Hamisham's house.

Sherlock Holmes and I, however, continued to favour cabs.

* The London metro is the oldest in the world, having opened in 1863.

** Holmes is apparently referring to the gang of juvenile Irregulars of Baker Street.

THE PHANTOM OF YORKSHIRE

While we resided together at 221B Baker Street, it was a common occurrence that cases simply came to Holmes of their own accord. He had merely to lounge on the sofa in our drawing room, and pick and choose the adventures or mysteries that would most stimulate his mind, relieve him of boredom and a dangerous lethargy*, and present a challenge for his brain. At this peak of his active career, there were so many telegrams, letters and messages that our postman often joked as to how much the Royal Mail would save if it opened an office directly in our building. The detective sorted the requests carefully, discarding the trivial ones immediately and using a penknife to pin those that appealed to him to the mantelpiece, after which he gradually dealt with them.

Our clients often paid a personal visit. I should note that not all of them were polite enough to arrive at certain unofficial office hours, let us say after breakfast and before supper, but this was understandable and excusable – they came to us seeking salvation, driven by fear or a sense of threat, not infrequently in matters of life or death, where every minute was crucial. We had become accustomed to being alert at all hours of the day, and our ears were trained to distinguish the thudding of footsteps hurrying up the few stairs to our rooms, even through the daily cacophony of sounds and bustle of the city. Nor was it uncommon for representatives of the police force to approach us with a request for advice, most often Inspector Lestrade.

As for letters, little changed after we moved house to *Cuckmere Haven* near Fulworth. The number of uninvited guests may have declined, and even Scotland Yard made an effort to respect the detective's retirement, which was only interrupted by the events surrounding the Great War.**

Yet there were a number of cases which interested Holmes for other reasons, persuading him to overcome his laziness to pursue them without having been asked for help by anyone at all. For instance, the events which I have recorded in my notes as "The Adventure of the Phantom of Yorkshire."

It was not I who invented the title – I copied from the sensation-seeking journalists who had written about the series of mysterious crimes in the county with such vigour that they soon attracted attention all across England. These were seemingly inexplicable burglaries of homes, individuals and families, usually in the dead of night when the occupants were at home but unable to impede the intruders and thieves in any manner – not because they were asleep, but because they were prevented from any physical movement by a mysterious invisible force.

"I cannot think what to make of it," I paused, wondering over the aforementioned wording. "An inability to move may be caused by ordinary fear or shock, when a person's muscles give out. I've witnessed it first-hand countless times," I mused.

"It is hardly likely that all the victims and their families would have the same panic reaction," disagreed Holmes, who had already read the papers but now reached for them again, returning to the article. "My personal guess would be hypnosis."

While I had experienced several incidents in which hypnosis had played a role during my time with the detective, I remained sceptical about such explanations, ranking them among the parlour tricks of stage magicians.

"It takes time and the ideal setting to induce genuine and effective hypnosis," I reminded him. "I should hardly think a burglar has the opportunity."

"I am speaking, naturally, of delayed hypnosis," Holmes chided me gently. "Not even I believe a burglar could break into somebody's bedroom and only there start dangling a pocket watch on a chain before their eyes while reciting incantations. But we cannot preclude the possibility that those afflicted had been exposed to hypnosis in the past, and the culprit now needed only a trigger mechanism. A signal, perhaps a sound or a word to reinduce a trance in the victims spontaneously."

He reread the text, as though hoping to discover new words hatched among those already used. "You are indeed right in that the wording is extraordinarily vague. The writer relies on patchy information and brief statements. He asks questions but does not seek any answers. He seems quite satisfied by the mere fact that a mystery exists," he added glumly.

Nevertheless, I noticed that he had not discarded the newspaper, but instead had extracted the page describing the incident, folded it up and tucked it into the pocket of his dressing gown. He was obviously intrigued and intended to follow the case. Over the course of the following days, he tended to be pensive at breakfast, dropping everything and riffling through the headlines rapidly as soon as the fresh newspapers arrived. He passed the evenings by the fireplace in silence with a drink, and if he did start a conversation, he mused over the Phantom rather than his usual chatter about beekeeping. I knew the urge to visit the scene was fighting with the feeling that he did not wish to impose himself on an investigation to which he had not been invited.

On the third day, however, the *Standard* brought a report about another case, embellished this time with sensational details and an in-depth interview with the victim, who was determined to divulge the entire experience to journals. Holmes's restraint was overcome, and without consulting me, he returned from his morning run of errands in the city with two train tickets.

Before noon, we found ourselves on our way to Pickering, a minor market town in the north, where this spate of unusual paralyses was taking pace.

We arrived at our destination late in the evening. First we took lodgings for the night, and in the morning, having gulped down his breakfast, the detective reported to the local police station. His concerns that they would turn up their noses at the offer of a helping hand from the famous detective were unfounded – on the contrary, it was gratefully accepted.

"The whole affair is reminiscent of an adventure novel by some fantasy writer, were it not for the fact that it is really happening, and in my town, no less," the chief inspector despaired. "There is growing panic and hysteria, and everybody is afraid," he admitted. The case was evidently beyond his abilities. The assistance and reinforcements promised by London had not arrived yet, and the terrified citizens had started organising their own patrols.

We were assigned a young constable named Lodge, and together set out to visit the victims. As we strode through the narrow streets of the town, overshadowed by the ancient castle on the hilltop, he described all that the local force had discovered up to that point.

It wasn't much. The investigations had found no clues in any of the houses.

"It is quite a conundrum. People are suspicious; paranoia has started spreading among them, and I can't say that I'm surprised. The homes in which they've always felt safe are at the mercy of an unknown power," Lodge concluded his report with undisguised concern. "It is a great relief that you've arrived when you have."

"I would prefer not to publicise my involvement too much for the time being. For one thing, I do not wish to alarm the culprit, nor do I want to raise false hopes," the detective tempered the constable's expectations.

"But surely you have a theory in mind, having come so far!"

"I regret you are mistaken. My interest was piqued by the bizarre nature of the affair, and I refuse to conjure any theories at all until I have obtained accurate and undistorted data directly from the interrogation. Were I to form a hypothesis based on those ludicrous articles and their allegations, the outcome would have to be a ghost, a member of an alien civilisation, or a supremely intelligent ape."

Holmes's dry humour did little to dispel the gloom. The young policeman fell silent and obediently led us to the house of Mr. and Mrs. Hardin, the Phantom's latest victims.

It was the gregarious Mr. Hardin who had been the subject of the article that had finally provoked Holmes to undertake the journey. He received us readily, ushering us into a cosy drawing room, and repeated his version of the events to us without any need for persuasion.

A few days ago, the elderly couple had awoken in the middle of the night, having heard a suspicious rustling from their bedroom on the second floor of the terraced house.

"My wife thought the cat had knocked something from the shelf, and was about to get up and take a look," recounted the gentleman, still agitated, wearing a house coat and slippers. He had a slight lisp because of his missing front teeth. "But she found herself unable to get out of bed. Her arms and legs wouldn't budge, it was as though she were paralysed. She couldn't even light the lamp on her bedside table. She started screaming in horror and woke me up."

"Were you able to rise?" Holmes asked.

"To tell you the truth, I don't know. More than anything, I was frightened," Hardin said, shamefaced. "I jerked, my head started spinning, I began to feel nauseous and briefly lost consciousness. It was as though somebody had thrown a sack over my head."

"An understandable physiological reaction at your age. Your pressure flew up, the blood rushed to your head, and you felt faint," I said reassuringly.

"How long were you unconscious?" the detective frowned.

"Only for a moment," the pensioner shuddered, recalling the experience again in his mind. "When I came to, my wife had started moving a bit and was crawling over the bed towards me."

"Adrenaline," I reasoned. "That, too, is common. Intense stress can release up to ten times the usual amount into the blood stream and the body – putting it in layman's terms – mobilises itself."

Hardin, however, was quite oblivious to me and carried on telling his story. "When we finally managed to get up from bed, we took a look around the house. The cat had been locked in the bathroom, and both the upstairs and downstairs were in disarray. Closets, drawers, everything was open, and things were strewn about the floor, locked drawers had been pried open."

"And the burglar was gone," Holmes observed. "Was anything missing?"

"Just some petty cash, which we keep at home for emergencies – otherwise we've got everything at the bank, thankfully. We are rather sorry about my wife's jewellery though," the man sighed.

It was enough to put my friend's brain in gear for the first time. He began systematically asking about details, thus eliminating dead ends of inquiry.

"I assume you were examined by a doctor?"

"Oh yes, we summoned a physician as soon as we'd received the report," Lodge straightened up like a ramrod in an effort to preserve a modicum of professional honour.

"The constable's right," Hardin lisped in support of the police officer. "Both my wife and I underwent a variety of examinations first thing in the morning. We are fine. I have no problems, apart from my teeth, that is – the dentist, Benton, is making me new ones. I had nothing but a headache, but that soon passed."

"Good to hear," the detective said approvingly. "Of course, what I meant was whether you have any traces on your body. Such as a puncture from an injection, which may have immobilised you while you were asleep, or perhaps a bump or bruise from a blow."

"We thought of that, too," the young policeman hastened to reply. "The doctor found nothing. Neither on the Hardins, nor on any of the previous victims."

"So be it," Holmes shrugged. "Yet what you have described suggests some kind of exotic poisoning. No external force can account for your immobility. I believe it was a temporary, artificially induced paralysis, and after a certain amount of time, feeling was simply restored to your limbs. The Phantom is not a murderer. I assume your stomach was pumped."

"Certainly not," the man shuddered in disgust imagining the procedure.

"Pity," I remarked regretfully. "It would be the only way to determine with certainty whether somebody had mixed something into your meal…"

Lodge withdrew a notepad and pencil from the breast pocket of his uniform.

"My apologies, I will take notes for next time," he said, leafing through it.

"Our task, Constable, is to ensure that there is no next time," the detective remarked, rather sternly. "I do hope you have at least secured all the foodstuffs."

"We have indeed," the policeman said repentantly. "Nothing unsound came of their analysis."

"And a sample of water from the well?"

"Yes, it is clean."

Holmes turned to the pensioner. "Where do you usually dine?"

"Why, at home," Hardin cried, almost offended. "My wife goes to market and the nearby shops every morning. Indeed, she is there this very moment, and knowing her, she is gossiping away with the women at the bakery or butcher's shop. She is an excellent cook!"

"Do you grow any vegetables or keep chickens?"

"Oh no, we are not keen on that. Our garden is purely ornamental."

The detective fell silent for a moment, straightening his thoughts.

"Have you and Mrs. Hardin attended the performance of a magician or conjurer recently?" I took advantage of the situation to inquire, having remembered our discussion earlier in the morning when we had stumbled onto this curious case.

The constable, still scribbling something in his notepad, halted, raised his eyes to mine, and together with Hardin and the detective himself, stared at me in astonishment. On the heels of Holmes's cannonade of rational question, mine must have seemed out of this world.

"No," the man cleared his through, embarrassed. "I do not venture out at all, not until my dentures are ready. My wife attends her ladies' book club, organised at the parish every Thursday by our mayor's wife. Oh, and she has Housey-Housey on Tuesdays."

"Satisfied, Inspector Watson?" Holmes teased me.

I pursed my lips, feeling I did not deserve this ridicule, for it was he, after all, who had first come up with the hypothesis of hypnosis.

By then, his reflections were far advanced.

Thankfully, he changed the topic. "You mentioned that you have a cat. It too was unharmed?"

At that moment, a large rusty tomcat leapt into Hardin's lap.

"Donald was fine," the owner scratched the cat behind its ears. "He was merely displeased at having been shut in."

Suddenly, something occurred to me that would logically fit the determined facts.

"A gas leak may cause similar symptoms," I blurted out.

This time, my words met with success.

"Excellent, Doctor! An accurate deduction, which I was likewise aiming towards," Holmes complimented me. "Was there any odour in the house?" he asked the owner.

Hardin could neither confirm nor refute this. "You see, my wife has been applying some sort of yeast mask to her face for years, so my sense of smell is rather dulled."

I imagined what a cosmetic treatment made of such ingredients must smell like, and suddenly the smoke from Holmes's pipes didn't seem quite so bad.

Lodge likewise made an attempt to repair his tarnished reputation. "We conducted an inspection of the gas lines and stove. Everything is tight, the valves were all closed."

"All right, all right," the detective grumbled.

"How about a gas or narcotic substance not originating from the household? We are in an industrial area – there are textile factories and other plants nearby that use all variety of chemicals. The wind may have carried the fumes in this direction," I said, developing my idea further, seeing as we had found no better explanation yet.

Holmes nodded solemnly. "Even I find such a thing possible, and even quite probable. Not least because gas rises to the ceiling, which is why the cat sleeping in a basket on the floor was not affected. But you forget that this was no accident. We are dealing with a deliberate poisoning and carefully chosen households. It is no leak, but cold-blooded intent. The Phantom of Pickering obviously has access to chemicals."

"Then we must check all the factories and their employees," Lodge paled at the thought of how many human souls and manufactories this could entail.

"But how would the gas reach us?" Hardin wondered. "Through a closed window, no less?"

"Why, it is summer," Holmes interjected. "Do you not ventilate?"

"The night was warm indeed, but my wife was frightened. After all, the burglar had already rampaged through our neighbourhood, striking Mrs. Dickens and Neville and Mimi Skipper. We've all been keeping our windows shut until they catch the scoundrel."

"Sound reasoning indeed."

"The chief inspector issued a recommendation to that effect," added the constable.

The detective looked around the room, and evidently concluded that there was nothing more to find here.

"Before we go, might I possibly take a look at your garden, through which the culprit got in," he asked Hardin, who led us, without objection, to the garden – it was really a narrow strip of grass on the other side of the house, bordered along the fence by a bed of flowers, shrubs and several mature trees.

"The ladder was propped against the wall so as to reach the window upstairs next to the bedroom," the owner pointed out the precise spot. By now, the place had been tidied up, much to my friend's displeasure.

Holmes studied the house and, head titled back, measured the height of the first floor.

"How did the Phantom get inside at all?"

"He pushed a thin wire through the crack to release the lock, and then slid up the window sash from the outside," the constable hastened to reply, so as not to be reprimanded for having neglected anything.

"Why climb upstairs when you have windows on the ground floor too?"

"Those on the ground floor were locked and shuttered," Hardin reasoned. "And I had left the ladder folded up in the garden but ready to use, as I am repairing the guttering," he admitted.

The detective shook his head at such carelessness, sighed miserably and proceeded to examine the lawn beneath the window where the ladder must have been positioned. Kneeling down, he rested his face on his arm and focussed on the neatly cropped blades of grass.

"There are pitifully few traces left now, days after the deed, as the grass has managed to right itself. Yet there are several visibly trampled and broken blades to be seen."

He then turned his attention to the soil.

"The earth is dry, but diligently watered, and the legs of the ladder have left an indent," he rejoiced. "Judging by its depth, I estimate that the Phantom weighs some nine and a half stone. He is therefore of slight physical stature, which fits the profile of a house burglar, who must be agile and lithe."

Holmes rose and dusted off his knees.

"Your bedroom window is the other one, about twelve feet to the right?" he ascertained.

"Yes," Hardin confirmed.

We moved beneath the other window, where my friend again spread himself over the grass.

"But this isn't where he got in," said Lodge in surprise. "You're wasting your time," he declared.

"Are you sure?" Holmes asked from the ground. "Then how do you explain that the ladder left the same marks beneath this window as it did below the other?"

The constable flushed and started stammering. "I… I… unless he wanted to make sure the Hardins were sleeping."

"Indeed," Holmes retorted. "Mr. Hardin, I need to visit your bedroom after all. Should my suspicions prove correct, we will have found the answer to the first part of this riddle, and a clue to identifying the perpetrator."

We ascended the wooden staircase inside and entered the old-fashioned bedroom. Lavender scented the air and the fierce summer sun shone through the lace curtains onto the rustic furniture. The closed windows made the room so hot and stuffy that I had to loosen my shirt collar.

Holmes pulled out his magnifying glass and, with the landlord's consent, strode directly to the window.

"Just as I expected," he exclaimed a moment later. He passed the handkerchief from his breast pocket over the lower part of the casing and windowsill. Several particles of sawdust stuck to it.

"I trust you do not have problems with woodworm…"

Hardin's eyes bulged and he shook his head.

The detective proffered his magnifying glass to the constable, inviting him to take a look.

"Upon close examination, you will find a minute opening in the bottom left of the window casing, no more than a few millimetres. It is easily missed at an ordinary glance."

"I can see it, too," Lodge exclaimed in surprise.

"It is so cleverly placed that you cannot see it unless you bend down. I imagine the burglar drilled it manually, as soon as the couple fell asleep, or perhaps even before they came up to the bedroom from downstairs. It only took a moment, but he was in no hurry, as it was dark and the view of the garden from beyond is obstructed by trees."

"And he let the gas in through the opening," I added the obvious.

"Quite so. I would say he inserted a small tube and then merely waited for the substance to take effect. I am certain that if you examine the other victims' houses once more, you find similar holes drilled in all of them."

"Why, this is appalling," I gasped.

"But it is essentially good news for the inhabitants of Pickering," said Holmes, rubbing his hands with satisfaction. "You can tell them that they no longer need to fear poisoning by food from their gardens or water from their wells. Now that we know how the Phantom paralyses his victims, we are one step closer to exposing him!"

* * *

In the course of the afternoon, without the constable at this point, we managed to call on the three other families that had been visited by the uninvited guest. We heard stories remarkably similar to that of the Hardins, differing only in minute details, none of which contradicted our suspected use of an unknown gas – quite the opposite. Indeed, the expected, cleverly chosen and thereby overlooked openings were found at all the crime scenes.

In one household, the substance had so thoroughly intoxicated the occupants that they slept through the burglary. Elsewhere, it resulted in paralysis or temporary crippling. Dorothy Dickens, a most attractive lady in her best years, reported symptoms similar to Mr. Hardin, namely dizziness, fainting and a brief loss of consciousness. Mr. Kearney even suffered a nosebleed, after having smelled an unknown, sweetish odour. All these difficulties disappeared after a few hours.

However, there was one other important detail in Mrs. Dickens's case, which caught our attention. When she had found, while in bed, that her limbs refused to move, like Mrs. Hardin she had started calling for help and had alerted her neighbours. From their windows, they had seen a figure dressed head to foot in black, scurrying from her property and escaping through the adjacent gardens into the darkness with some kind of sack slung over his back. It was the first and only time the Phantom had been seen to date. We were pleased to hear that the description matched Holmes's initial estimate as to the culprit's height and weight.

The day ended with an evening meeting of Pickering residents at the town hall, which had been convened by Mayor Burton because of the recent crime wave. Several hundred inhabitants gathered in the great hall, including Burton and his councillors, the physicians Benton and Fishburn, and seated on the podium was our acquaintance Chief Constable Robins, facing a barrage of discontent from the crowd.

He might not have plucked up the courage to speak to his fellow citizens at all, had my friend not taken him aside and whispered something to him briefly beforehand. Robins then announced that the famous Sherlock Holmes had been summoned to the town at his initiative, and was on the brink of solving the case in close cooperation with the constabulary. He then recounted all that the detective had allowed him to present.

As expected, the inhabitants calmed down upon learning precisely what they were facing. They were visibly relieved to discover what causes the paralysis and how, and the mystery suddenly became somewhat less terrifying.

It was replaced with indignation and the Phantom of Yorkshire was promptly given a new nickname – the Mad Gasman. Burton then thanked Holmes and urged his fellow citizens to give the detective their fullest cooperation. Nevertheless, we kept the details of what direction our investigations had taken to ourselves.

The detective took advantage of the meeting at the town hall to speak with the remaining owners of the burgled houses whom we had not had the chance to visit in person during the day.

Among the last of them were Neville and Mimi Skipper, the younger couple previously mentioned by Mr. Hardin, but we learned nothing relevant from them – perhaps because they were presently at odds over Mr. Skipper's alleged infidelity, of which his wife had accused him in public.

"I cannot tolerate his escapades any longer!" Mrs. Skipper cried, unable to restrain her jealousy any longer and, quite contrary to social convention, launching into a tirade against her husband in front of us and a group of onlookers. "Always smelling of a different ladies' perfume! Heaven only knows where he cavorts with them while neglecting his family!"

The small town would have yet another hot topic to discuss in the coming days.

"The woman is mad," Skipper defended himself, trying to calm his wife down.

But there was no escaping the embarrassment, as his spouse was only just getting into her stride.

"Mr. Holmes, I will pay you any sum you ask if you provide me with evidence," she urged my friend, who was struggling to terminate the conversation as swiftly as possible.

"My apologies, madam, but I leave this type of detective work to others," he said in an attempt to extricate himself.

"Why Mimi, I promised you last time that it was over with all of them. I've been behaving ever since," Skipper cooed. "She's been going on like this for days," he explained to us apologetically. "She even knocked my tooth out last time!"

"I don't believe a word of it," lamented Mrs. Skipper. "Instead of staying home with me after the burglary, he took off again and got back God only knows when! They were doubtless canoodling somewhere. The whole house smelled of that wench!"

Holmes quickened, understanding suddenly.

"Given what I've heard, I might take the liberty of offering an explanation," he said, unable to suppress a mild smirk. "What you smelled at home may have been the residue of that gas, which has a sweetish odour. It would be a logical explanation."

The alibi offered by Britain's greatest detective perked Skipper up.

"I swear I wasn't with anybody! I went to the police station and argued with Robins, telling him that his people were lazy and that I would escalate the affair," he sought to persuade his wife.

She hesitated. "You menfolk always stick together," she continued to scowl at her husband.

Fortunately, we were rescued from the raging marital spat by Lodge, who had returned in the midst of the conversation. Nevertheless, he confirmed Skipper's visit to the police station, quelling the argument for the time being. Out of the couple's earshot, he whispered to us that Mrs. Skipper's husband interpreted the sanctity of wedlock very loosely indeed, and that he – as a police officer accustomed to spending much time in the field – was convinced that her suspicions were not unfounded.

He then added that the mayor wished to speak to us.

We were only too happy to extricate ourselves and moved away to see Mr. Burton, who wanted to thank Holmes in person – that is, only for his efforts made so far. On the occasion, we were introduced to both of the town's physicians – the general practitioner Dr. Fishburn and the dentist Dr. Benton, who were also on the town council.

While Holmes and Fishburn engaged in a professional debate on the potential consequences of gas poisoning, I addressed Benton and his charming companion, unsure at first whether she was his young wife or daughter. I did not think the slender, fair-haired creature suited the older, stocky gentleman with a pince-nez and whiskers, although I count myself among those who believe in true love and affection deeper than the fleeting intoxication of superficial beauty.

Instead, Benton introduced the young lady as his medical nurse and assistant.

"How do you do, Doctor," she said, lightly and timidly extending a lace-gloved hand.

I pressed it gently, noticing its intoxicating scent.

"I've always said the loveliest flowers grow here in the north," I complimented her.

She flushed slightly and lowered her eyes.

"I would be obliged to arrest you without mercy for plucking this particular flower, Doctor. It is a protected species," said Lodge, placing a protective hand on her shoulder.

"Edward, darling," she welcomed him with a kiss.

"Miss Ellie Reed and I are to be married," the young man beamed at me joyously.

"Then I wish you only the very best," I congratulated the enamoured pair.

Benton looked considerably less benevolent. He gave the constable a stern glance and stepped between the young couple with such force that he quite literally pushed Lodge aside with his paunch, forcing the constable to take several steps sideways. Then the local dentist withdrew his pocket watch and frowned at it meaningfully.

"It is high time we left, Miss Reed. It is almost the twenty-third hour, and our patients will be awaiting us in the morning," he reminded her.

The young lady nodded and Holmes, who had come to bid his farewell, gallantly helped her into the dress jacket she had placed over the back of a chair in the hall.

"Shall I see you tomorrow?" the constable asked.

She managed to whisper that they would meet at the usual time, before Benton hurried her away.

"A charming beauty," I remarked.

"Thank you," the constable smiled.

"Doctor Benton, on the other hand, does not seem to be the best companion," Holmes interposed, watching the pair depart. The dentist stepped out with an air of self-importance, while Ellie trotted obediently after him, leaving behind only the scent of her perfume.

"He is fairly new in town, having replaced the deceased Doctor Mitchum but a few years ago, shortly after the war. He hasn't fitted into local society very well, but people do praise his professionalism. He is fast, precise and inexpensive," Lodge admitted. "Perhaps that is why he was recently elected to the council. Ellie, on the other hand, has been the town's darling from the outset. Benton brought her with him, and I fell in love with her at first sight. To her, he is like the father she doesn't have. They met during the war at an infirmary somewhere, where she was nursing the injured and he served as a physician. She has seen so much horror in her life that she only deserves happiness from now on. Once we've married and saved up, we would like to go to America."

"Bold plans indeed!" I exclaimed.

"People should have grand objectives. It makes it easier to achieve smaller ones in pursuit of their fulfilment," my friend agreed, patting the constable on the shoulder encouragingly.

Meanwhile, the meeting at the town hall had broken up, the residents of Pickering had returned to their homes, and we were the only ones remaining in the hall.

We were in no hurry, for there was a long night before us. A small office was put at our disposal to make ourselves comfortable, with refreshments prepared by the mayor's secretary awaiting us.

The next part of our investigation was to take place here.

All afternoon and early evening, the constable had been busy with a task assigned by Holmes, to collect information about all the establishments in an around Pickering that use chemical substances. The detective intended to have all the available details before embarking on a personal inspection of all the sites tomorrow. For somebody with the soul of a chemist like my friend, it was a dream assignment, but for the constable it was a veritable nightmare.

North Yorkshire is known for wool processing, as well as producing fabrics for the clothing industry in general. However, the array of required chemicals was enough to make even the detective's head spin.

"Gases are formed by thermal decomposition and naturally have different effects and properties, depending on the different formulas, ratios and compounds. Our man must be an expert with proper equipment. He knows exactly what he is doing and what he needs," Holmes mused as he perused the compiled file. Fortunately, the relevant municipal administration department had all the information we could possibly need. "Regrettably, we do not know exactly what gas the Phantom or Mad Gasman, if you will, is using. We do know that it is characterised by a sweetish odour, so it may be some derivative of nitrous oxide, which you will know from your medical practice as laughing gas or diazoxide."

"But that has only anaesthetic effects, it does not cause paralysis!" I pointed out.

"Which is why I am speaking of some derivative substance," the detective emphasised. "There are plenty to choose from," he ran his finger over the list of substances on the sheet. "Various kinds of acids used in the garment industry, for example, sulphuric, hydrochloric, or acetic, lead dyes, cadmium for setting them, as well as alkalis, a variety of reagents, detergents, chlorine, formaldehyde, and on and on. I would have to be in my laboratory to conduct a series of experiments to determine exactly how each compound behaves," he mused.

"Best to sleep on it then," I suggested, for I could feel my thought processes slowing down as weariness came on.

"You are right, my friend," Holmes folded up the documents. "Today has been quite eventful and tomorrow will be no less demanding. Constable, I assume you have some mode of transport at your disposal. Please pick us up at nine o'clock," he asked Lodge.

With these words we parted, and the detective and I walked from the town hall to our boarding house, Holmes taking the opportunity to smoke a pipe in the pleasant balmy night air. I did not distract him, for I knew that flashing before his eyes were not the picturesque little houses of Pickering, but instead complex chemical formulae and the interactions and reactions of compounds.

* * *

As instructed, the constable collected us precisely on time, a fact appreciated more by Holmes than myself. Although the detective fell asleep long after me and rose much earlier, he appeared far more refreshed, driven by his desire to solve the mystery and tear the mask from the face of the elusive Phantom, who was being hunted by the entire town.

Our inspection started at a small enterprise on the outskirts of town, where wool was cut, sorted, combed, washed and dyed. Several chemicals were used here, but all were industrially processed; there was no in-house laboratory or opportunity to work with them any further. They were also stored as per safety regulations. We stayed only a short time and moved on.

All the greater was our astonishment at the next, rather larger textile production factory, for the chief technologist, with access to an amply supplied warehouse, was none other than Mr. Skipper.

"But that is no secret, I've been working here for ten years now," he laughed nervously at our surprise. "You didn't ask me about it yesterday, and it didn't occur to me that it might be important."

"An interesting coincidence," said Holmes, gazing around the factory hall full of clanging weaving machines, apparently operated mainly by women.

The perfect setting for an adulterer.

"What exactly is your occupation, Mr. Skipper?" the detective inquired. "Naturally, I am only interested in the part that concerns work with chemicals."

"I specialise in dyes, sir. My people and I are constantly improving their composition, colour fastness and permanence," the technologist explained.

"So you have the necessary chemical engineering expertise," my friend ascertained.

"Of course," Skipper confirmed, without realising that at that moment, the admission played against him.

As did I, Holmes ran his eyes over the man's slight figure, perfectly matching the description of the pursued criminal. "Were we to ask your wife about the evenings on which you were allegedly unfaithful, would they by chance coincide with the nights on which the Phantom attacked?"

"I don't like where your questions are going, sir," objected Skipper, once it had dawned on him. "Have you forgotten that my wife and I were also attacked?"

"You would certainly not be among the first to furnish an alibi by feigning an attack on yourself," the detective retorted icily. From behind him, Lodge gazed searchingly at Skipper – like us, it had not hitherto occurred to him that the culprit could be hiding in plain sight.

Holmes asked Skipper to remain available for further questioning, whereupon we left the factory and returned to the car. The clock showed it was time for lunch.

"Do you really suspect Neville?" the constable could not help wondering.

"He has the means and the expertise. What's more, he must finance his little escapades somehow, so he would have a motive," Holmes replied drily. "Unlike you, my dear constable, we are not encumbered by the blindness that prevents you, as a local, from seeing certain things for what they really are."

Lodge nodded, took the observation to heart, and opened the motorcar door for us.

"I say, my friend, I think it would do no harm for Doctor Watson and I to have luncheon somewhere nearby," the detective surprised us instead. "Lodge, please return to the station and inform your chief that we are about to close the case and reveal the Phantom. Tonight, he will be convicted and arrested in front of everyone at the town hall."

"Are you certain?" Lodge paused, the memory fresh in his mind that barely twenty-four hours ago, Holmes had not wished to inspire any false hopes.

"The only certainty is that the sun will set," my friend remarked cryptically. He hurriedly wrote a few lines on a paper napkin and folded it up. "Give this to him with my message, and come back for us as soon as you can. We have yet to carry on, our search is far from over."

The bewildered constable set off to town to spread the important news, and we found an inn nearby, where we enjoyed some respite and a good meal.

"It is obvious to me that you see something that I do not, but I would like to know how you want to prove that Skipper is the Phantom," I pondered. "All we have is indirect evidence and conjecture. We don't even have the laboratory where he produced the gas."

"I have certain ideas about where that laboratory is located, and about the origin of the Phantom's gas," said Holmes, savouring his roast and home-made bread.

We were, once again, playing his favourite game of withholding his deductions until the final moment. He often said it was a way to give me more time to solve the case on my own, but this happened only very seldom. Still, I have learned to wait patiently and not pry for further details.

Lodge returned about an hour and a half later. As per Holmes's wishes, he had delivered the message to Robins, who had surely informed Burton and the councillors, and convened another meeting over the town loudspeaker by now.

"Is this wise?" I asked, concerned. "What if we are wrong?"

"It is essential," the detective dismissed my fears. "Constable, at what time does the train depart for London?"

"Four o'clock in the afternoon," Lodge replied, his eyes bulging. "You're not going to leave, are you?"

"No indeed," said Holmes, starting for the car and hurrying us along. "Nevertheless, we must catch that train at any price!"

Hence, we scrambled into the motor, the constable stepped hard on the accelerator, and we sped down country lanes, through the suburbs and industrial areas of Pickering, to the town centre. The car engine roared so loudly that we were unable to say anything more. I merely understood from a few words that Holmes intended to confront somebody at the train station.

The railway station at Pickering is also the terminus of the North Yorkshire Railway, and is a relatively small building with a single floor and two platforms, one for arrivals and the other for departures.

Lodge pulled up abruptly in front of the entrance, but Holmes remained seated, perfectly calm.

"I deduced what you're up to on the way here!" he exclaimed excitedly. "You wanted to frighten Skipper into attempting an escape, isn't that so? You're hoping that after your confrontation, he'll have headed straight to the station, thus incriminating himself!"

The detective smiled, but sadly. "If the information you carried travelled precisely as I expect, our Phantom is indeed pacing nervously about the platform, hoping to disappear as swiftly as possible," he confirmed the police officer's surmise. "But I must warn you, my dear constable, that it is not Mr. Skipper you will find there."

"Oh, you don't say!" he cried, readying the handcuffs as he dashed inside.

Holmes and I followed him at a slower pace. Before we reached him, my friend had time to prepare me for what I would unfortunately bear witness to.

"Had I told the poor lovesick chap beforehand who would be at the station, he most likely wouldn't have believed me, and might even have warned them," he sighed.

Waiting on the platform were Miss Ellie Reed and Doctor Benton, both carrying only the barest essentials for baggage.

Lodge stood at some little distance before them, as though transformed into stone.

"Are you going somewhere, love? You never mentioned anything," he stammered, confused. Any number of thoughts must have been whirling through his head. "Why, we've got a rendezvous tonight…"

Ellie bit her lip anxiously and Benton's eyes twitched in search of potential escape routes, but with his gainly stature, even I might have caught up to him.

"If I may give you some advice, do not attempt to shoot your way out. The station is surrounded," Holmes warned him. "I trust that you, as a physician, will honour the Hippocratic oath even in your present situation. Incidentally, you have already shown that you have no desire to kill."

Benton growled, but did not seem bound to attack us.

"I don't understand," Lodge swallowed hollowly. "Ellie, what on earth is going on?"

As she did not reply, my friend spoke for her.

"You are standing before the twofold Phantom of Yorkshire, or perhaps the Mad Gasman, my dear chap. But the word "mad" is inappropriate. Greedy is more to the point, and most likely a deserter, too," Holmes declared, revealing the pair.

"Deserter?" I exclaimed in astonishment. "You are an army doctor?" I looked at Benton. He, however, chose to remain silent.

"He is indeed, but he serves a different majesty than you do, Watson," Holmes continued. "Mr. Benton and Miss Ellie are German spies, who stayed on in our country after the Great War. Their empire lost, and they had no choice but to remain here in secret. Disguised as a respected physician and his assistant, they won the confidence of the people of Pickering, he as a councillor and she through a calculating relationship with a young police officer. This ensured a source of local information, making them feel safe and concealed."

"That is a rather bold allegation," remarked Lodge, unconvinced, still hoping it was all a mistake.

"No indeed, merely a series of logical conclusions. Perhaps you could ask the young lady to present her travel documents. As a police officer, you are entitled to do so."

The constable extended his hand to Miss Ellie, as though in a trance, yet quite uncompromising.

By then, reinforcements had arrived at the train station, led by Robins himself.

Ellie could but obediently withdraw her own and Benson's documents from her purse. They were made out under entirely different names, but forged so masterfully that nobody would ever notice.

They fell from Lodge's limp hands.

Holmes picked them up and peered at them. "Just as I thought," he said.

The chief constable was the first to find his bearings among the startled police officers.

"Doctor, Miss, I would like to believe that all this will be duly explained, but for now I must ask you to accompany me to the station," he instructed. "We will take care of your luggage."

"Do not forget to examine the suitcases," the detective said. "They contain the Phantom's loot."

Lodge crouched down to Benton's suitcase and opened it in front of us all. It was full of jewellery and other small valuables, as well as bundles of cash.

No further evidence was needed.

"I hereby arrest you," he said, grasping his fiancée by the arm, perhaps more brusquely that appropriate. "Anything you say henceforth may be used against you."

Robins's men took care of the rest and led the ensnared pair away to the police car.

We sat with the devastated Lodge on an empty bench and watched the last passengers board the train, having provided them with quite the distraction while waiting for its departure. The conductor blew the whistle, the engine blew steam and slowly pulled away from Pickering station.

"I, too, would have succumbed to that beautiful face, at your age," I comforted him. "Not everybody is a born lie-detector like Holmes here."

"It's not that I was suspicious of Miss Ellie – or whatever her name is – in particular," the detective said defensively. "I was merely toying from the outset with the idea that the Phantom could be a woman. I was led to this assumption by the burglar's estimated weight, and it was confirmed by Mrs. Skipper's conviction that she could smell her husband's mistresses in the house the following day. Women do have a particularly keen sense of smell, far more developed than men. Yet even we noticed how lovely and distinctive Miss Ellie's scent was. Her perfume pervaded the entire town hall. It occurred to me that a woman like her may have left this trail of scent behind during the burglary. Had it been the residue of gas, something I told Mrs. Mimi merely to rid us of her demands to spy on her husband, Skipper would have had a headache. I considered it a merciful lie," he admitted.

So that's what he was pondering over so deeply as we strolled back from the town hall meeting that night! He must surely have begun to suspect even then. "Very well, but what about the other things?"

"The Phantom handled the gas with considerable skill, not just in terms of chemical engineering, but also from a medicinal perspective. Nitrous oxide is commonly used during more complex interventions also by dentists, and many of the victims had suffered dental problems in recent months. This drew my attention to Benton. He has plenty of equipment at his surgery to work with gases, which Robins is sure to find on examination. Incidentally, his laboratory was on your list of places where volatile substances are stored," he reminded Lodge. "Do forgive the obfuscation – I wanted Benton to stew in his own juices and attempt a hasty escape in his panic."

"And that they are Germans – spies even?"

"There are several minute pieces of evidence to that effect. For instance, that Ellie wears German-style clothing. When they were leaving the town hall, Miss Reed gave Benton priority at the door. As a woman, albeit his subordinate, she should be shown deference, but they automatically behaved like soldiers, where the higher rank has the upper hand. It was no ordinary lack of tact or proper manners, merely habit. And even you heard Benton refer to the eleventh hour of the evening as the twenty-third. The twenty-four hour format is used on only the Continent and particularly in the army. I suppose they had originally been deployed here to conduct experiments on our population using the gas the Emperor's secret service had equipped them with."

"It is true that experiments using gas as a biological weapon were started by the members of the Triple Alliance," I said, recalling the shocking case of 1917 when the Germans first employed this tactic during an attack in Yprés. Their first gases destroyed the respiratory passages and actually burned the lungs. The version Benton had tested in Pickering, though more merciful, would have proved tremendously effective in a military operation.

"If they were indeed spies, they made a fatal mistake by drawing such attention to themselves," Lodge muttered.

"Which is why I am convinced that they betrayed their service to their nation. Instead of using the gas inconspicuously and as far as possible from their place of residence, they opted for a highly risky undertaking. They needed to amass a fortune as quickly as possible, in order to then depart together, I believe, for America to begin a new life. That was the only part of the plan Miss Ellie was truthful about," the detective concluded his analysis of the crime.

"I was living somebody else's dream," sobbed the constable.

"That is why it is important to have one's own dreams," Holmes said, as we all three left the station, side by side. "I, for instance, am dreaming of a peaceful evening at home on the sofa."

"That is a dream I share with you, Holmes, despite your advice," I laughed.

It was not until we were back at the farm that the news reached us that the gas found in Benton's abandoned laboratory had been received with high expectations by the British military intelligence, which immediately subjected the unknown substance to thorough examination.

Its potential military use by an enemy against Britain thus lost any strategic effect.

To celebrate our victory, Holmes invited me to London to see a performance by one of the world's most famous hypnotists.

* The danger Watson is alluding to must be the detective's inclination to use opiates. See "Sherlock Holmes and Golem's Shadow."

** See "Sherlock Holmes. His Last Bow."

FLAMES
FROM NOWHERE

Of all the possible ways to take the life of one's fellow man, I consider fire to be the most repulsive. Any violent death is horrific and tragic – indeed the infamous Whitechapel murders* will remain before my eyes until I draw my last breath – but as a physician, I know how slowly and painfully flames kill. Slashing, stabbing and firearms, if handled properly, can kill instantaneously, but fire suggests that the arsonist enjoys watching his victims suffer, like a beast toying with its prey.

In my opinion, no living being deserves to burn.

Not even Sir Roger Singleton, to be sure.

Had we not been nearly trampled by a speeding horse-drawn fire engine, equipped with hose and manual pump and festooned with firemen in blue uniforms, while crossing the street near our lodgings, we might have noticed his name in the newspapers only on the following day, where his mysterious death would certainly have occupied considerable space with headlines several inches tall. Instead, the naturally inquisitive Holmes set off immediately in the direction of the speeding fire engine, followed by a gaggle of children clamouring for cool shower on a hot day. I, of course, went with him.

The loud clanging of the bell calling for help brought together an excited crowd, which converged just a few corners down from a multi-storey office building that housed a number of businesses – the largest being a certain shipping company. According to a prominent metal sign, partially obscured by a mature plane tree at the edge of the pavement, its offices occupied the third floor.

To my surprise, however, the fire brigade had not yet begun untangling the hoses and the fire hydrant was still intact when we arrived at the site a few minutes later. In spite of their previous haste, the firefighters were now sitting awkwardly on the fire engine's footboards, and it was clear from their spotless uniforms that they had not yet attempted to tame the flames.

Their commander stumbled out of the open door of the house, removed his shiny helmet and wiped his sweaty brow with his sleeve. He was pale and exchanged a frightened glance with the constable, who was fighting to hold back the sensation-seeking, shouting crowd of onlookers, which continued to swell.

Holmes and I pushed forward.

"I've never seen anything like it before," the fireman said, his voice constricted with terror.

"I took but a little peep inside and dared not go any further," the constable nodded. "I'd rather stay down here and wait until the men from the commissioner's office arrive."

My friend glanced back at me stealthily and raised his eyebrows.

"Come along, Watson, I'm becoming rather curious," he beckoned, elbowing his way towards the officer.

"What has happened here?" Holmes addressed him with natural authority.

The man, like most police officers in London at that time, knew Holmes well and was aware of his contribution to the suppression of crime and maintenance of public welfare in general. Moreover, he was visibly relieved to see somebody with experience on the scene, so he addressed the detective as if he were his superior.

"Good afternoon, Mr. Holmes," he saluted. "There was a call from the house a few minutes ago that there was a fire, so I summoned the fire brigade."

"And why aren't they do anything? Why don't they put it out?" I inquired.

"Because... it was no ordinary... fire," the policeman said haltingly, avoiding our gaze.

"Could you please be more specific?" Holmes frowned.

The poor fellow was rigid with fright. "It wasn't a house fire or anything like that...," he swallowed hollowly. "I ran briskly up to the third floor, opened the door, and there... was... Sir Roger burning up... I'm afraid he's beyond help."

His words sent shivers up my spine. The detective, on the other hand, perceiving the possibility of an interesting case, was able to fully suppress any excess of sensibility.

"Might we take a look upstairs?" he inquired almost eagerly.

The police officer pointed us to the storey in question, insisting in a trembling voice that it was essential for him to remain below and maintain order on the street. We did not object, seeing his horror at the mere idea of returning to the scene.

Holmes and I ascended to the shipping company offices alone.

In the entrance hall, dominated by a majestic life-size portrait of the proprietor, we found the secretary slumped on the sofa for visitors. In a state of utter shock and incapable of speech for the moment, she stared at the open door of the owner's study with protruding eyes. A small man with gartered sleeves, who appeared himself to be in need professional help, was attempting to comfort her, albeit without great success. The other employees, mostly made up of women – typists, sat nervously at their desks in the work cubicles.

Intuitively, the detective strode to the door, but as he reached for the handle to open it, he hissed.

"Be careful, Doctor, it is still hot," he warned me, lest I too should burn myself, and he drew a silk handkerchief from his breast pocket with which he opened the double doors.

The secretary whimpered and buried her face in her colleague's waistcoat, so as not to see anything more.

Indeed, the horrific sight that presented itself was not for the faint of heart.

Sir Roger, or what was left of him, was smouldering in the armchair beneath the window.

There was the partially burned torso of a stocky male figure. The fire had consumed him sitting up, while the lower half of his body was surprisingly well preserved. His legs from the knees down were relatively undamaged, attired in the trousers of an expensive pinstriped suit and beige spats over his shoes.

Very little remained of the upper half of the body, on the other hand. The torso had been burned to a crisp, leaving several very ragged cracks. The skin had fused with the clothes, and there was no face left to speak of. It had melted as though it were made of wax, the bare skull exposed in several places. The charred arms hung limply alongside the body, barely remaining attached at the shoulders, yet the palms and the manicured fingers with their massive rings were intact.

The armchair, which barely held together, was also destroyed, as was the side table standing next to it, with a pair of charred and ruined spectacles. The floor in the immediate vicinity was cracked with heat. Greasy ashes flew about in the air with a lingering odour of burnt flesh. The rest of the room was in remarkable order, and apart from the omnipresent soot, there was no sign of the tragedy that had taken place.

"Do not touch any metal objects, they are only just cooling," Holmes warned me.

I had seen many scorched scenes of fire and mutilated bodies, but never I had seen flames target a single object in this manner. It was as if they cared for nothing else and needed only to feed on their victim. Or as if someone had set them deliberately...

"Please open the window and air the place out," the detective requested, handing me his handkerchief to cover my mouth and nose. He did not need it.

While he examined the dead man closely, I stepped over to the window, under which lay several fallen black cinders and scraps of paper, turned the handle and opened it wide to give fresh air to my lungs.

"Remarkable," muttered Holmes, fascinated. "At first sight, it looks as though the fire ignited around the stomach and consumed the poor fellow at once."

We looked around, but saw nothing that could have caused such a blaze.

There was merely a discarded blanket laying on the floor near the door, which had been used to extinguish Sir Roger. On the desk were a writing pad and utensils, a jar of emollient cream, a crystal decanter of brandy two-thirds empty and two short-stemmed glasses, one of which was cracked.

"He was having a drink with someone here. Most likely with the murderer," I said, pointing to the decanter.

The detective examined it, then returned it to its place, and knelt down gingerly beside the chair, where he blew away the ashes and studied the remains of the dead man's hands and feet closely.

"He did not put up any struggle at all. Had he twitched or attempted to run, he would have scraped the floor with his soles of his shoes. But he seems not to have even noticed what was happening."

"He must have been unconscious," I reasoned.

"Yes, that is certainly one possible deduction," Holmes smiled. "There are no charred remains of rope, so he was not physically restrained."

"What a bizarre way to murder a person," I sighed.

"We must first identify the origin or cause of the fire," Holmes said reluctantly. "Only then can we determine with certainty how Singleton died. However, I agree that it was not spontaneous combustion."

He was alluding to the fanciful superstition, so appealing to journalists, that arose from time to time in cases of unexplained fires. The idea that fire could originate in the human body without an apparent source of combustion was first put forward in the summer of 1746 by one Paul Rolli, a fellow of the Royal Society, in the journal *Philosophical Transactions*. His treatise dealt with the mysterious death of the Italian Countess Cornelia Zangheri Bandi, whose maid had found only a pile of soot and three fingers in her place in the bed.**

As in the case of the poor noblewoman, there was nothing here from which the fire could have originated. There was no hearth with burning embers or candles in the room, nor, judging by the absence of smoking paraphernalia, did Sir Roger indulge in the habit, and as the building was lit by electricity, no kerosene lamps were used.

"Let us speak to the staff, we may be wiser then," he suggested, whereupon we returned to the lobby of the company's offices, where a sombre atmosphere prevailed.

The diminutive accountant, who had been comforting the female clerks, moved to speak.

"Miss Fitzpatrick knocked on Sir Roger's door at three o'clock to tell him that she was leaving for the post office, as she did every afternoon," the man said eagerly. The position of his desk allowed him a fine view over the entire office.

The young woman, still shaking from the shock of her experience, blinked and nodded.

"Then I reached for the door handle, but it was all hot," she piped softly.

"I pushed the door open and saw what was happening. Miss Fitzpatrick shouted 'Fire!!' and I threw a blanket over the gentleman to smother the flames, but it was no use," added the accountant.

Holmes measured the accountant and the other ladies with a stern look.

"Who visited Sir Roger during the morning?"

"Nobody," the secretary shook her head. "His diary for today was blank, he wasn't supposed to have any appointments or meetings. He was locked in there by himself all day."

I cannot speak for my friend, but I myself was puzzled.

"What happened in that study is definitely not a suicide," Holmes pointed to the door. "Yet you say no one else went in?"

"I've been sitting outside his door since morning; indeed, I haven't even taken luncheon," she confided, as if our doubts had infused energy into her veins. "But we are eight of us here in the office. If you don't believe me, ask the others!" she exclaimed defensively.

"I can confirm that," the little man chimed in, standing up for the lady. "Even if Gladys had popped out, there were seven other pairs of eyes on Sir Roger's door. No one was here."

"I am not suggesting that I don't believe you," the detective assured her. "I am merely ascertaining the facts."

"There is a decanter on the desk that is almost empty. He must have drunk it with someone," I remarked.

Fitzpatrick blew her nose loudly. "It was full only last night, I refilled it myself," she marvelled. "The gentleman insisted on it, and it was the last thing I did every night."

The detective continued to deliberate.

"Did either of you hear the sound of a scuffle from the study? Anything strange?"

"Nothing at all."

It was only now that Holmes showed any exasperation. "It takes several hours to char a body in that manner. I find it difficult to believe you failed to notice a fire blazing in the adjacent room."

The accountant let out an agonised groan. "It is the height of summer, a hot day – indeed the hottest of the year – and it never occurred to anyone that the heat could be from anything else," he threw up his hands. "Besides, the windows are open, there's plenty of bustle outside, the typists are always chattering inside and tapping away at their machines. We really heard nothing else."

"Nor did you smell anything burning?" I said, frowning.

"My dear sir, we live in central London. We're accustomed to any variety of odours."

I had to admit that his reasoning was quite sound.

The detective's aggravation, which he tended to show when the solution to a mystery eluded to him, abated, and he proceeded to speak to the accountant and ladies more gently.

He paced about the office, pausing at various points to look back at the door. He examined what could be seen from each position and under what conditions. He exchanged a few words with each of the distraught typists and asked them not to leave quite yet. Among other things, they all confirmed that their employer was not a smoker, and like us, none of them had the least idea what could have caused the fire.

"When was the last time you saw Sir Roger?" Holmes asked when he returned after a moment to the central pair.

"It must have been around eight o'clock, when he came into the office," said Miss Fitzpatrick.

"What kind of spirits was he in?"

"Poor," admitted the secretary, "but, with all due respect, that was not out of the ordinary with him of late. He instructed us that he did not wish to be disturbed, and merely assigned us our tasks."

"Are you aware of any troubles, any motive, or how anyone could benefit from Sir Roger's death? I must know everything, even those details which you may find seemingly unimportant."

The accountant loosened the collar of his shirt and shrugged.

"There are many such people," he sighed. "As Gladys intimated, Mr. Singleton has recently been involved in a number of business disputes, some of which are certain to end up before the courts, and, without wishing to be indiscreet, he had no reason to be happy at home."

Despite the stoic expression Holmes had assumed, I noticed that the last statement piqued his interest.

"His son had decided to go to America and start a business there, refusing to take over the family enterprise," explained the accountant, who had sensed the same keenness.

With this, however, the spark in Holmes's eyes faded away.

"So it was not in his interest to inherit the business now and attach himself to London," he reflected, scratching off the gentleman's son as a suspect in his mind.

I assumed that we would now follow the trail of the aforementioned business disputes. It made sense to me. Singleton might have received his adversary in secret, shared a drink or two, but reached no agreement; on the contrary, the feud had escalated and this heinous murder had been committed. But how the perpetrator had come and gone unnoticed, by what means he had committed the attack, and how it was that no one had heard anything outside the study door, I was truly at a loss to understand.

Yet I was certain that if anyone could solve the mystery, it would be Sherlock Holmes.

He stood in the middle of the room, listening intently to the sounds within and without. He closed his eyes. From the street came the noise and chatter of curious onlookers.

"The investigators from the Yard are still nowhere in sight, but a whole throng of reporters are here already," the detective observed, leaning against the sill and glancing briefly out the window.

He looked around for a moment, shading his eyes as he peered at something in the distance, perhaps on the roof of the building across the street, and then, as if struck by a sudden thought, he turned back into the room.

"Watson, you opened the window when we entered Sir Roger's study, did you not?"

"Yes, you asked me to do so yourself," I reminded him.

"Had it been closed before?" he lashed out at the accountant.

"No, it had been open," the man blinked. "I closed it, for I did not want prying eyes from the house opposite or from the rooftop looking in."

Holmes clapped his hands. "Why did you not mention it before, man? It changes the situation entirely!"

He strode briskly into Singleton's study and headed straight for the window.

"It should have occurred to me immediately," he exclaimed, pointing to the black-rimmed scraps of paper on the floor beneath the window next to the table with the spectacles. He picked them up, examined them, and replaced them carefully. "The draft must have blown them about when Fitzpatrick opened the door!"

"Do you suppose someone threw something into the room?" I guessed at his line of reasoning.

The detective opened the window wide. The branches of the plane tree spread out a few feet before him.

"It is obvious," I answered myself. "Someone climbed up here and threw an incendiary device or explosive at Sir Roger!" I rejoiced at having discovered the solution.

Yet I received not praise, but a critical analysis of my speculations.

"Then the murderer must have been a trained monkey or rickety child," Holmes chided. "Observe the thickness of those branches. They could not possibly bear the weight of any man I know. And the thicker ones nearer the trunk grow at such an angle that you could not see through the window from them. The blast of an explosive would be heard both indoors and on the street. Besides, plenty of people would have seen such an attacker, for we are on a busy thoroughfare. And Sir

Roger would have easily shaken off any other conventional flammable material and fled from the window."

There was a whole battery of arguments against my reasoning, and it fell it to pieces.

"Then who set Sir Roger on fire, and how?" I exclaimed.

"Wait here, Watson. I am sure you will have your answer presently."

He walked solemnly round the charred body of Sir Roger, past the accountant and the ladies waiting at the door, requested their patience, and hurried away. A moment later, I saw him dash from the building, weave his way through the crowd to the trunk of the plane tree, and examine its surface with a magnifying glass.

He then returned to the house.

I ran to the staircase eagerly to meet him.

"I checked, for the sake of your peace of mind, but no one has been up that tree," he called to me as he ascended the stairs. "The bark of the trunk is quite intact."

"Then we are back where we started," I said with disappointment.

Yet, unlike me, Holmes was no longer groping in the dark for an answer.

I could tell by the slight smile with which he gazed into the crown of the plane tree.

By then we had retreated again to the study, where we found peace away from the curious employees – Holmes intended to acquaint them with the results of his investigation only after he had arranged his thoughts and reported his findings to the police inspectors.

He was already in the process of summarising a full report for the latter.

"It is not always necessary to seek sensation and complexity where there is none. You already know that," he began deliberately, sitting down on the window casing and fiddling with his magnifying glass. "After all, it is usually quite elementary, my dear Watson..."

"You must admit that a number of our cases have, on the contrary, been rather complicated."

"Quite so, but I always start from the simplest explanations in my deductions," he exclaimed. "Please be so kind as to recapitulate for me exactly how, from a medical perspective, death by burning occurs," he requested in a friendly manner.

I shuddered at the very thought.

"Well, the victim first begins to suffocate," I strove not to be overly suggestive. "He is prevented from breathing by the hot smoke, which burns the airways. The combustion produces carbon dioxide, which soon renders the individual unconscious, and besides that also carbon monoxide, a deadly poisonous gas, which then kills. The question remains, however, whether the shock of the body's nerve endings being subjected to excruciating pain may occur sooner. As a result, the blood pressure drops, the internal organs shut down and death occurs."

As I have already mentioned, I know of no crueller way to die.

Holmes held up a finger. "And that answers one part of your question."

"I do not follow."

"Sir Roger was entirely incapable of defending himself from the fire. For he had drunken himself into a stupor, and when the flames blazed up, he inhaled the fumes in his sleep, and never woke up again."

"But he did not get intoxicated on his own!" I exclaimed, still searching to defend at least a part of my theory. "There are two glasses on the table! Someone must have been with him."

"There are indeed two glasses, but he drank from both of them," the detective announced. "It makes sense. The first glass is cracked – he may have struck it inadvertently, and I believe he spilled the spirit onto his clothing. So he took a new one. In any case, he drank all morning, dissatisfied with his situation, perusing his papers over and over, searching for loopholes, until drunken sleep overcame him. After all, he was able to endure a great deal with his constitution."

"How can you be so sure?"

"I examined them. Sir Roger took great care of his hands and applied cream to them. I found traces of it on the bottom of both glasses as he warmed them in his hands."

Slowly, the meaning of his words dawned on me.

"So it was not murder?" I sputtered.

"I am absolutely certain it was not."

"Then, pray tell, how do you explain his spontaneous combustion?" I dared not breathe with anticipation. "Did a ball of lightning fly into the study? Or have you started believing in pyromaniac spirits?"

Holmes did not answer immediately, but continued to hold up the magnifying glass, which glittered in the sunlight.

At first I thought he was hesitating over how to put his thoughts into words, but then the dry sheet of paper on the table next to the armchair began to smoulder, and a moment later a tiny flame appeared.

"Sir Roger fell asleep in the armchair next to the open window, his waistcoat soaked with alcohol. He had put down his papers and removed his spectacles automatically shortly beforehand. The portrait in the hall shows him without them, so I judge that he wore them for reading only – he was farsighted. I am certain his staff will confirm this. He placed them on the table beside the armchair, which is situated beneath the window, so they are within arm's reach. The laws of optics and a very cruel fate took care of the rest," he stated. "For his reading spectacles have convex lenses, which are thicker in the middle than at the edges."

The lens of the spectacles had previously, just as Holmes's magnifying glass with its convex lens had now, amplified the effects of the morning sunlight and, when positioned at the right angle, actually had the power to ignite a fire. By cruel accident, Singleton had tossed aside his spectacles so that they landed on the side table, intensifying the refraction of the incoming light beams with their focal length. The alcohol-soaked linen waistcoat then served as the tinder and reagent.

"If you look outside, you will notice that the sun – like in our own rooms – illuminates this room in the morning, whereas now it is slowly receding behind the trees," he pointed out the window. "This is a prime example of being in the wrong place at the wrong time."

The events that must have occurred here that morning unfolded before my eyes.

Yet Holmes's bold hypothesis answered all the established facts beyond any doubt – the fire that had burned only half the body, and the fact that the rest of the study had remained intact. It had only heated the air enough to warm the metal door handle.

One could compare it to a burning candle wick***. Sir Roger's garments had started to burn, but before the pain could rouse him, the poisonous fumes from the fire had intoxicated him. As soon as the flames had breached his skin, the heat began to dissolve the subcutaneous fat, which then seeped and was absorbed into the fabric, nourishing the fire for several hours. For even an ordinary human body contains many pounds of fat, let alone the body of a stout shipping magnate. The flames then burn in an upward direction and do not fan out. As for the legs and arms, they contain the least fat, and were hanging downward, thus being spared.

I shuddered in disgust.

Indeed, there is no death more cruel than that by burning, but in this case I was glad there was no human agent behind the incident whose soul was so corrupt as to plan and execute so horrible a murder. No, this case was nothing like the rampage of the Cornish arsonist we had encountered a year before****.

At last the footsteps of the police investigators could be heard outside the door, and Inspector Lestrade burst into the study. His eyes protruded from their sockets upon seeing the charred torso of Sir Roger, and he clearly went to some effort to keep his stomach from turning. Having noticed us, however, he fought to maintain decorum.

"You're here already?" he greeted us, staring helplessly at the havoc around us. "Well, I wonder how we're going to solve this one. The chaps downstairs said it was a mystery."

Holmes glanced discreetly at his pocket watch.

A mere thirty minutes had elapsed since our arrival.

He gave Lestrade and his men precisely the same amount of time before delivering his explanation.

* Dr Watson appears to be referring to Jack the Ripper's rampage, which claimed the lives of many women.

** This case did indeed take place in Cesena, Italy, in 1731.

*** In modern crime fiction, it is actually called the wick effect.

**** Notes on this case have not yet been discovered.

THE ADVENTURE OF THE

FORGOTTEN DONATELLO

I've always felt better about publishing my accounts of curious robberies and burglaries than those concerning some poor soul's death or even murder. Truth be told, especially in the early days of my literary career, recounting particularly tragic cases made me feel that I was preying on someone else's misfortune. It took Mr. Doyle – with help from Sherlock Holmes – some time to talk me out of it. Even then, I always endeavoured to present as varied an array of cases as possible to those interested in my friend's work, rather than clouding their minds with naught but morbidities.

Looking at my selection of cases for this volume so far, I believe it is high time for a change of tone. A case comes to mind in this connection, which we encountered during one of our sojourns in sunny Italy.

In this context, it is important first off to point out that although Holmes and I have visited a great swathe of the world, our travels were never of the short or holiday type. The detective was not one to indulge in the touristic pursuit of the seven wonders of the world, and his idea of respite was limited to the divan by our hearth, a pipe and a full tobacco pouch. When he did venture outside of London, or even beyond the borders of England, the journey was always strictly expedient. Although he ignored the call of Hermes* with icy calm, he could never resist the lure of an interesting crime or mystery.

Yet our sojourn in Capri was on other grounds entirely. Following a particularly involved and exhausting investigation, which need not be specified herein, Holmes needed to recuperate both physically and mentally. Our mutual friend, the physician who kept up my practice whenever I was unable fully to attend to it, emphatically recommended that Holmes spend at least two weeks somewhere warm, with plenty of fresh air and most importantly, as he stressed, in peace. Holmes would have none of it at first, but as I too felt the need to shake off the recent tension, together we managed to persuade him.

Two weeks of travel beyond England seemed to me not only an excellent idea, but indeed a prerequisite for such a holiday to make any sense at all. For one thing, it was practically impossible to find a place in our homeland where temperatures would exceed ten degrees at that time of year, and for another, it was only beyond the country's borders that the detective could hope to find at least some degree of anonymity.

The Isle of Capri, situated at the lower end of the Apennine Peninsula, appealed to us not only for its beautiful scenery and diverse flora, but also because there was an exceptional artistic masterpiece on display at the moment – a recently discovered work by the famed Renaissance sculptor Donatello, a bronze nude figure of an antique warrior about eight inches in height.

This is, at least, what they claimed in *The Illustrated London News*, which I opened during a delicious breakfast of home-made apple pie and compote, faithfully brought to us by Mrs. Hudson. The illustration next the article immortalised forever the owner and the finder of the statuette, two pompous Italians with beaming smiles.

"I do take the liberty of correcting the author of the text, however," Holmes called to me from behind the closed door of his bedroom, just as I had finished reading the article. "That statuette was not newly discovered, it has merely been newly attributed to Donatello. Be that as it may, it is a fantastic achievement, and I would rather like to see it before they move it from the private collection, where it was found, to a depository where it will be studied by scholars, only to be shown to the public again many years hence."

As he had not yet left his room that morning, I could not fail to wonder how he could tell, through the wall, what I was doing, which newspaper I was reading, and even which article I had just beheld.

He had even guessed this unspoken thought of mine.

"Judging by the vigorous clink with which you put down your teacup, I gather you are wondering how I could possibly know what you are leafing through at this very moment," he laughed with amusement from a distance. "It's elementary. Before retiring to our bedrooms last night, you arranged the newspapers on the table from the most recent to the oldest, as per your fastidious nature. *The Illustrated London News* was delivered yesterday afternoon, and I managed to read it in the early evening, whereas you saved it to read at breakfast, which is why you placed it on top. After all our years of cohabitation and the countless instances we have spent together, I know precisely how fast you read, and because I heard you pouring out the tea and rustling the pages you were about to read only a few moments ago, I deduced the exact time when you were likely to reach the end of the article at the bottom of the front page. Am I right?"

As always, after he had performed a similar stunt, I had nothing whatsoever to add.

That very day, desiring to refresh not only our bodies but also our souls, we purchased train tickets to Naples, and three days later we found ourselves aboard the first morning ferry to Capri, a small island in the Bay of Naples, along with a group of noisy and boisterous Italian youths heading to the same destination.

"Perhaps we were foolish to expect to find the peace needed to rest in Italy, let alone in its southern regions. We can only hope that the recommended lodgings are sufficiently secluded," Holmes sighed, as the ferry approached the picturesque harbour of Marina Grande, nestled in a natural bay with high cliffs rising up on either side.

Chaos reigned supreme here too, but not because of the Italian temperament – it was because of a crime!

The members of the local carabinieri boarded the ferry as soon as it had docked and, after a stormy discussion with the ship's captain, announced to all the passengers that no one would be allowed to disembark.

With my limited knowledge of Italian, I had grasped that the island had just been closed off.

One of the youths, about whom I had clearly formed a mistaken opinion, turned out to be a capable interpreter into English and willingly offered us his assistance.

"A work of art of incalculable value was stolen here during the night, and the police refuse to allow anyone to leave or enter the island until the entire matter has been resolved," he translated the words of the garrulous policeman. "They are hoping the culprit has not yet left the island, and they are conducting a thorough search."

It was fairly obvious that he was talking about the Donatello statue.

"And where is the Navy?" inquired the detective, scanning the horizon doubtfully. He saw nothing in the azure waters around us. "Because without them, they will have a hard time indeed controlling the movement of private vessels in the surrounding waters."

There was another excited exchange of melodic words, accompanied by theatrical gesticulation.

"There are supposedly patrols with binoculars all along the coast, monitoring the traffic at sea. If they spot a vessel departing without authorisation, they will dispatch a motor launch to pursue it," our interpreter informed us.

This time, Holmes kept his disdain to himself and politely, albeit without any room for objections, asked to meet with whomever was in charge of the search.

"But what about your holiday?" I grumbled discontentedly, disappointed that we had failed to evade work even here.

"Let us be honest with ourselves, Watson," my friend grinned. "My work is my hobby, and cracking a theft like this would be as soothing to my nerves as relaxing baths and massages. Possibly even more so!"

I will not dwell on the chain of lower and – if not in stature then in rank – higher officers we were obliged successively to muddle through, but before long we were presented to the young, dark-haired commander of the garrison, dressed in an overly embellished dark blue uniform with piping, red lampasses and highly polished boots. Holmes muttered under his breath that such attire was appropriate at best for conducting an investigation at an amusement park, but outwardly put on a sweet smile. Fortunately, the carabiniere was not lacking in sagacity and linguistic facility, and no interpreter was needed. He also proved to be aware of Holmes's reputation, and quickly understood that the famous detective's involvement in the case significantly increased the chances of a prompt resolution.

The detective prodded him further. "We are on an island with more than ten thousand inhabitants and countless tourists, scattered over an area of approximately six square miles. In such conditions, searching for a small statuette is comparable to looking for a needle in a haystack. The investigation must be conducted with the utmost professionalism."

"There is only a squad of orderly police permanently stationed on the island," the commander admitted in shame. "The detectives and criminal investigators from Naples have yet to arrive. The gallery owner reported the theft only a while ago, and closing off the island seemed to me the best solution!"

"Allow me to offer you my services, in the hope that by the time your colleagues arrive, the case will be solved," said Holmes, with a slight bow. "I shall be happy to leave all the credit to you."

The little man's arms shot up into the air as he thanked the gods in his native tongue for sending this aid, and he bade his men to arrange for our transport to the scene of the crime.

We set off up a winding road to the higher reaches of the island, whose principal city shared its name. The historic centre of Capri was situated on a sort of plateau overlooking the sea. The island itself, as far as the eye could see, was covered in a carpet of colourful flowers that gave it the moniker "flower island." If I were a painter, I might not have a colour palette adequate to capturing everything realistically.

We alighted from the carriage with a police officer in front of the Grand Hotel Quisisana in Piazza Umberto I. The square was dominated by a tall clock tower, and the traditional morning market with vegetables, fish and other fresh food was in full swing, the air permeated with a mixture of distinctive aromas.

On the way here, we had gone through all the available information.

For generations, the statuette had belonged to the private collection of Signore Montesutti's family, one of the oldest on the island with roots dating back to the 14th century, when the island was first settled. Until recently, the creator of the artwork was uncertain, but a recent expert opinion had attributed it to Donatello. It is a fact that, after leaving his native Florence, he had worked in many places across Italy, including Siena, Pisa, Rome, the Vatican and Naples, where he had carved a remarkable tombstone. During his stay in Naples in the first half of the 15th century, the artist had apparently spent some time in Capri as a guest of Montesutti's ancestors, and clearly did not idle the time away with folded hands.

Following the discovery, the family's current patriarch Alessandro Montesutti, a prominent Italian billionaire and philanthropist, decided to donate the statue to the Museo e Gallerie Nazionali di Capodimonte in Naples, but as a patriot of Capri, demanded that it first be put on display for several weeks at a local gallery, where it could be admired by the inhabitants and visitors to the island.

The carabinieri officer provided us with the latest news.

The gallery was located on the ground floor of Signore Montesutti's villa right here on the square, with the rest of the house occupied by his extended family. The gallery, like the entire building and extensive grounds, is under surveillance around the clock, but the thief had overcome the guards. The man patrolling the very hall where the statue was located was found unconscious and handcuffed in the early hours of the morning. The Donatello, of course, had disappeared.

"Who found the guard?"

"Signora Montesutti."

"The wife of the master of the house?"

"The elder sister," the policeman specified. "Signore Alessandro is a widower, raising an only daughter, Ellena. His sister, Louisa-Maria, moved in years ago after she herself was also widowed. She has a son, Giacomo, whom Signore Montesutti has practically adopted. As far as I know, the family lives in complete harmony."

"I would like to speak to them. Who else was in the house last night?" Holmes inquired.

"Besides the servants, only a representative of the museum and an agent of the insurance company. Both institutions were somewhat uneasy when Signore Montesutti clung to his intention of exhibiting the statue here, without proper security. They therefore insisted on the constant presence of their people. Quite rightly, as it turns out."

"Indeed," replied the detective, allowing himself to be ushered without further delay into the gallery in the white plastered two-storey house built in the Mediterranean style.

He was interested in speaking to the assaulted guard first.

The distraught man, guarded by a rank-and-file carabiniere, was squatting on a chair near the entrance, a wet rag pressed against his forehead. Over his shoulder, I could peer into the halls filled with private collections, several interconnecting rooms replete with paintings by Old Masters and display cases of various objects. In the middle of one of the smaller rooms, on a low stone, stood another, slightly taller pedestal of pinkish marble with a polished round surface, now sadly empty. A door, fitted with a lock, led from the gallery to the private quarters of the house.

Likewise, there was only one window into these rooms, that being the very room in which we were standing.

It was ajar. Apparently, this was how the thief, or thieves, had entered. Holmes's attention was drawn immediately to the pile of shards on the floor under the sill, and the hole in the glass pane.

The carabiniere had already described it carefully in his notebook. "The burglar – probably with a diamond cutter – cut a hole in the glass from the outside, thrust his hand through it, and quietly opened the window. He then crept in, probably hiding behind one of the cabinets, and ambushed the watchman as he passed by, knocking him out."

"How many men were in charge of security?"

"Two. One inside the hall and one with a dog outside on the grounds."

"And they saw no one?"

"They had no suspicions until the alarm was raised. Not even the dog barked."

"Let us believe they did not fall asleep, and that it was most likely a very quiet burglar," Holmes said, focusing on the gaping hole in the glass. First he examined it closely with his hand, and then ran his finger lightly over its sharp inner edge.

"The cut out piece of glass has been broken. Perhaps the thief accidentally kicked it as he climbed out. He was in a hurry, carrying the precious statue, and may have wavered slightly with it," the policeman reasoned. "Whatever the case, the guard didn't hear the sound of shattering glass, so it must have happened while he was unconscious."

"I'm delighted to hear you've included logic in your arsenal," the detective complimented him. "There are, of course, several possibilities as to why the robber first carefully cut out the pane and then broke it, but I see no reason why this deduction should not be included among the investigative alternatives."

Was I the only one who heard doubt in his voice?

The carabiniere, however, nodded self-importantly and turned to the guard waiting to be questioned. Yet Holmes made no rush towards the latter, remaining instead by the window and studying the frame, the sill, the handle, even opening it wide and leaning out. A narrow walkway of pebbled paving encircled the entire perimeter of the house, bordered by a carefully trimmed lawn.

"Yes, you can see the footprints outside the window all the way from here; someone was indeed kneeling and lurking here," he conceded. "The grass has since been covered with dew and almost righted itself, so we won't find any more clues. The direction he came from is not clear."

Then he looked up and gazed at the windows on the upper floor.

"I need to know whose windows open onto this side of the garden," he added.

The officer who had led us to the spot ordered his man to gather the other occupants of the villa while Holmes questioned the watchman.

As he was about to close the window, the detective's eyes noticed something in the grass.

He threw his leg nimbly over the sill and swung himself out into the garden.

"As you can see, there is little difficulty getting in or out of the house swiftly once the window has been opened," he remarked on his exercise as he bent down to the lawn.

A small shard of glass glistened in the grass.

When my friend presented it to the officer, the latter merely shrugged. "There's nothing strange about the shards falling on either side of the window when they shatter."

"In any case, it does put the lie to the theory that the thief broke the glass during his careless escape. There is no way a single shard from the floor inside could have just flown over the windowsill a yard high and fallen out into the garden."

"What do you make of it?"

"I'm not sure yet. Let's wait," the detective admitted. "Now, I would like to finally meet our guard. Let us see what his statement brings."

The carabiniere took the role of interpreter.

In my view, however, it was merely a retelling of everything we already knew. Although the detective occasionally interrupted the guard's description of events and asked for details, I had not yet seen the spark of understanding in his eyes, which always indicated to me that he was near to finding a solution.

What irritated the detective most was that the guard had heard nothing.

"The night was so quiet that even the cicadas could be heard from outside," the man argued through the mouth of our interpreter. "No footsteps, no doors opening, no glass breaking."

"Sometimes even the most trifling details can give us a clue..." Holmes pursued patiently, trying to refresh the man's memory, dulled by the monotonous work. "Are you sure you heard nothing strange? Breathing? The rustling of clothes?"

"Maybe... but I told your colleagues," the guard hesitated. "Just before I lost consciousness, there was something behind me. It was as if someone had stepped on a twig..."

"Yes, we have that on record," the officer agreed. "We searched the room carefully and there was no twig, broken or whole. It was cleaned last night, and if the burglar had brought anything in on his boots, he carried it away again."

Holmes rubbed his chin.

"Interesting," he murmured, his eyes darting back to the window. I gathered that he was examining every growing thing in the garden that such a twig might have come from. Ornamental shrubs, cypresses and other trees abounded. In my mind's eye, I could already see us picking our way through the thicket, looking for broken branches in the hope that a piece of clothing or other trace had got caught on them. Gloom was about to befall me, for it would have been a full day's labour. Instead, the detective shook his head and dismissed the matter for now.

"We shall see," he mused aloud. "Anything could have made that sound."

He picked up one of the shards from the window, placed it on the floor, and stood on it.

The shard cracked beneath his sole.

"Could that have been it?" he asked the guard, but the latter shook his head.

"It wasn't so sharp a sound. More muffled, like a crack."

The detective strode to the door of the house and grabbed the handle. It clicked, but the door did not open.

"It wasn't the handle or the lock either," the guard swore.

Holmes, dissatisfied with yet another failing of his ideas, pursed his lips.

"Well then, we are at a standstill for the present," he concluded, turning to the officer. "I shall need this man again. Allow him to rest, but do not let him leave just yet. Now, please take me to the Montesutti family."

The drawing room on the first floor, where we were already awaited, could be reached either directly from the gallery, which was connected to the house via the door already mentioned and presently locked, and more commonly through the main entrance to the house up a broad staircase leading from the hall to the upper floor which, besides the drawing room, also contained the private quarters.

We were escorted to meet the family by a sulky housekeeper who, far more than by the theft of a precious artifact, was annoyed by the fact that someone had made a mess of her pantry, and who insisted that we put on felt slippers because of the freshly polished floor. She had a whole pile of them ready in the hall.

There was an understandable air of nervousness in the drawing room.

The morning sun painted a picturesque scene outside the French windows leading to the terrace, which offered a breathtaking view of the bay. Yet the azure sea and green carpets of vegetation in the background vied for our attention with the luxuriously opulent furnishings of the interior and its inhabitants.

The faces of the six individuals present were gloomy.

It was obvious at first glance who the master of the house was. Alessandro Montesutti, whom I already knew from an accurate likeness in *The Illustrated London News*, embodied dignity itself; with his grizzled temples and thick hair he was, even at his age, the prototype of the Roman athletes who stood as models for the sculptors of antiquity.

His sister Louisa-Maria had surely had coal-black hair in her youth, and even at her ripe old age, dressed in a simple black widow's dress, she had a fire in her – now sadly dampened by visible woes.

Young Ellena might certainly have been a beautiful girl and quite her father's daughter had she not had a shy, almost fearful look on her face. Judging by her tanned skin, she liked to spend time outdoors.

Giacomo, about seventeen years old, had a few more pounds on him than would suit a boy his age, but he gazed at us with a proud and haughty look.

The other two men present were not members of the family, but guests who had been deployed to guard the treasure, in which their respective institutions were eminently interested. A stern insurance agent, who introduced himself as Marco Salestro, and the shorter, stouter representative of the Capodimonte Museum, Steffano Rossi.

To our relief, everyone's education included a knowledge of English.

"A rich reward awaits you if you help find the statue," the owner said in greeting.

"I am certain our museum will join in," added Rossi, in whom I recognised the other man from the newspaper. His round face was beaded with perspiration from the heat and anxiety, and he was constantly playing with his fingers, either because of his frayed nerves or perhaps because he didn't know what to do with his hands. "It is an incalculable loss!"

"Mr. Rossi of the Neapolitan Museum was the one who discovered the Donatello," Signore Montesutti confirmed. "We are, of course, at your full disposal."

"Is essence, I would like to discuss the events of last night and anything else you may have noticed," Holmes accepted the proffered seat and a glass of water.

"I am distraught about it myself, but cannot think of anything that might be helpful," Montesutti said.

"But surely you cannot speak for all," said the detective. "What about your daughter and nephew, perhaps they were out for a night's entertainment and noticed something on their return?"

"My daughter does not go among the local youth, much less at night," objected the master of the house. "I cannot imagine what she could possibly have to say to them. I love this island, but I want something better for her. She has studied in Switzerland, and when she marries she will most likely live in Rome or Paris. The world will be at her feet," he boasted.

"Si, padre," Ellena squeaked, staring at her hands clasped tightly in her lap.

Giacomo rolled his eyes.

"Uncle has a life plan in place for all of us," he drawled wryly.

His mother put her hand on her chest in indignation. "Apologise immediately!" she ordered her son.

His pout became even more pronounced, but he obediently uttered a few words. Montesutti patted him on the head condescendingly and commented with something about the rashness of youth, which he must beware of, because without his guidance it would grow like weeds.

"Is anything else missing besides the Donatello statue?" Holmes changed the subject.

Signore Salestro of the insurance company took it up.

"No, only the main exhibit. In our opinion, the thief acted with deliberation and did not bother, Signore Montesutti will surely forgive me, with trifles. Even so, the damage is incalculable."

"How much was the work insured for?"

The insurance agent whispered the sum in Holmes's ear, and the detective's eyebrows shot up. "A very pretty sum indeed."

"That is why we initially protested that the statue be displayed here, but the company's management eventually decided to grant an exception, if basic security measures were met."

"Two guards – is that not insufficient?"

"There is virtually no crime on the island, it seemed adequate..."

"Until you advertised the exhibit in the press around the world, of course," Holmes sighed.

"The timing was indeed unfortunate, but in a week the statue should have been safe in the museum vault," admitted a consternated Rossi. "After the battle, everyone is a general."

"I am not here to lecture or criticise you," the detective apologised, "but to attempt to help you. Now, if you will permit, I would like to look over the grounds and the rest of the villa."

***

Holmes and I spent about two hours walking about the house, and the detective also concentrated on its acoustics – where a sound was coming from and at what intensity. We looked out of the individual windows into the garden. It turned out that the window above the one through which the burglar had entered the villa belonged to the apartment of Signora Louisa-Maria, but she said she had been asleep all night and had seen nothing and no one.

"A pity, for it is your window that offers the best view of the south garden," the detective said regretfully.

"I take valerian drops for sleeping," said the widow, pointing to the bedside table, where stood a jar and a bottle of medicine. "With those, not even a gunshot would wake me."

"Fortunately, there is no need to test that theory because no one has died. I have, however, investigated cases where guards have been murdered for a far less precious loot," the detective pointed out.

Louisa-Maria crossed herself. "You don't say! This thief wasn't out for blood!"

We descended from the widow's room into the gardens, measuring the distances and the time it took the guard to traverse the various routes around the large estate. Then we returned to the house to meet its other occupants and observe their behaviour.

We also spent some time with Steffano Rossi, as Holmes was interested in how his discovery had come about. "There had been legends about the existence of such a statue in the area for years," recounted the fidgety historian. "So I systematically approached all the major local collectors. You see, several huge fires have ravaged the island over the centuries, destroying many documents and archives. Moreover, the Montesutti family was struck by the plague in the sixteenth century and nearly died out, leaving no survivors who knew the ancient origins of the collections."

"How tragic," I remarked.

"That is why Signore Alessandro is so anxious that his daughter should marry well. For three centuries, the family has carried the stigma of consistently preserving the family line."

Listening to Rossi, I felt some pity for young Ellena, whose father was seeking a suitable groom for her. Still, Alessandro Montesutti impressed me.

He received us in his study, which was overflowing with antiques.

Yet again, he offered us nothing that would advance our search. He explained that his bedroom had windows facing the other garden, and he could therefore neither see nor hear what was happening on the other side. "It's a shame my sister took those bloody drops. She had only recently complained that they weren't good for her stomach and that she wouldn't take them again. But Giacomo is a worry sometimes, so she probably wanted to get a good night's sleep. It's good for the nerves."

Holmes nodded. "I see," he murmured. "Well, I suppose you can convene the rest of your family and friends to the parlour. I do believe our investigation is coming to a close."

***

Holmes made himself comfortable in an armchair and lit a pipe. Only once he was certain that he had the attention of everyone present did he genially blow out some smoke and begin speaking.

"The first thing I would recommend," he said, turning to our faithful guide, the carabinieri officer, "is to open the harbour and end the blockade of the island forthwith. It is time to end the chaos and stop confining the inhabitants."

The latter looked surprised. "But what if the thief escapes with the statue?"

The detective shook his head and pronounced a crucial judgment.

"I think not. I am convinced that the statue is still in this house," he declared.

"I beg your pardon?" I exclaimed in wonder, while the others exchanged equally perplexed glances.

Even the carabiniere looked as though he had doubts as to whether bringing Holmes into the case was a good idea. "Do you think the thief broke into the house and left the loot here?"

"I would put it differently," said the detective. "I believe the villa was never broken into, that the culprit is one of the occupants, and that the statue has not in fact disappeared at all."

The expressed allegation had the effect of fireworks being thrown among the members of the household and their guests. A heated, typically Italian discussion broke out, in which everybody started getting angry, shouting, waving their hands, and gradually turning their attention to Holmes, whom they accused of being mad.

He did not bat an eyelid, however, and continued puffing on his pipe calmly while watching the spectacle he had unleashed with the amusement of a circus spectator.

"What an insult to my *famiglia*!" Montesutti hissed. "How did such insolence ever occur to you?"

"Thanks to the evidence," the detective assured him.

"What evidence?"

"Let us take it one step at a time. Might I know who holds the keys to the door which connects the house with the gallery?"

"Only I," frowned the don. "I confiscated all the others because the insurance people and the museum demanded it. They are kept in my study."

"Very well," Holmes again bade those present to be quiet. The noise level obediently dropped to a level at which his voice could assert itself, allowing the detective to present the demanded chain of his deductions and observations.

"Even at first glance, there was something odd about the cut out pane of glass and the pile of shards beneath the window. Indeed, it may have happened, but still... A closer examination of the cut in the window set off an alarm in my head. When cutting glass, the angle of the cut will never be horizontal, but bevelled, depending on the height you are cutting the glass from. The angle here clearly indicates that the glass had been cut from the inside, where the floor is significantly higher compared to the ground outside. In order to achieve the same angle from the outside, the perpetrator would have had to have a stepladder, which was impossible given the frequent rounds by the watchman."

"What about the glass under the window?" I asked, trying to follow his train of thought.

"My guess is that the perpetrator simply dropped it in his haste and it shattered," the detective surmised. "But not until the guard was unconscious, in any case. The sequence of events was as follows. The burglar entered the gallery from the house via the connecting door, to which he had procured the keys. It could have been anyone who knew where Signore Alessandro had left them in the study. He probably unlocked the door earlier in the day to avoid the sound of the lock turning in the night. It would have been no problem for any of the occupants of the house. He slipped in wearing a pair of those omnipresent slippers, so his footsteps couldn't be heard, stunned the security guard, and staged the scene to look like a break-in from the outside while the other guard was on the far side of the estate. But it didn't go quite according to plan. When the glass fell from his nervous hands onto the gravel walkway, the opposite side from where he needed it, he had to sneak back into the closet for a broom and dustpan and swing outside, where he quickly collected the shards – except for that one piece that bounced away into the grass and couldn't be seen – and dumped them inside. However, he failed to replace the equipment quite exactly as it had been, which angered the maid that morning. He wasn't a professional, but was merely pretending to be one."

Montesutti did not seem convinced. "I am no criminal expert, so I cannot judge the relevance of such a story," he said, looking questioningly at the insurance agent. The latter nodded silently, indicating that it did have some logic.

"If we were to accept the thesis that the perpetrator came from inside the house, it narrows down the number of suspects to those having this debate. In such cases, motive tends to be the detective's springboard, but any one of you could have had one. This little group has many secrets," Holmes swept a knowing glance over the assembly.

"I have no idea what you are talking about. I know everything that goes on in the family," frowned Signore Alessandro.

"I shall be glad to reveal certain other things to you, but I warn you beforehand, you may not like it."

"Do tell – what motive would my daughter have, for instance?" He waved a dismissive hand towards Ellena. "She has everything, she will inherit all my property, I deny her nothing!"

"There is something, after all... Miss Ellena is secretly married to someone of whom you disapprove, and as she cannot hope for a dowry, surely some other provision would suit her to begin a new life."

Ellena gasped and looked about to faint; Montesutti seemed ready to suffer another stroke.

"What?" he cried.

"I know I am putting you in a precarious position, but the truth would have come out soon enough anyway," Holmes apologised to the pale, bleary-eyed girl. "You have the deepest respect for your father, yet you cannot evade love. Every now and then you gaze dreamily at the ring finger of your left hand, where a strip of pale skin stands out against the tan. When your father can't see it, you wear your wedding ring, which you take off in his presence."

"Is it true?" the master of the house inquired angrily.

Something in Ellena gave way. "Yes, it's true. I've been married to Matteo from the harbour for several months. I'm sorry if I've disappointed you, father, but I cannot help it."

Alessandro rubbed the bridge of his nose in agitation.

"My daughter has married a fisherman," he wailed. "A man without a single penny!"

"But your sister and her son could also have a motive," continued the detective mercilessly.

Giacomo rose from his seat in annoyance. "Enough! I will not suffer such disgrace!"

Holmes was never impressed by shouting and threats. "Surely you will not deny that you have a problem with your uncle. It oozes from your every pore. Although your mother is older than he, Signore Allesandro is the head of the family who makes the decisions. You disagreed with his donating the statue to the museum, did you not?"

Louisa-Maria bowed her head, and even Giacomo finally gave vent to his hidden defiance.

"The statue is not just my uncle's to give away. It is the property of the whole family! He had no right to do it!"

Montesutti, mentally exhausted by the unexpected rebellion of both daughter and nephew, sat down in frustration. "But I am raising you as my own, boy..."

"I don't want to be another piece on your chessboard and accept your charity! I just want what my mother is entitled to as the eldest child!" Giacomo exclaimed.

Holmes gave the family no respite and continued with the onslaught of accusations. "As for Signora Louisa-Maria, I am certain she lied about having been sleep. She withheld the fact that she had seen somebody in the garden after being awakened by the tinkling of glass on the pebbles. I attribute this to an understandable maternal desire to protect her son, whom she herself suspects."

"But I am innocent!" Giacomo exclaimed in anguish. "Do you truly believe that, mother?"

Signora Montesutti hid her face in her trembling hands.

"I... I... it's true, I wasn't asleep. Something disturbed me, and as I looked out, I saw someone who reminded me of you. I'm not sure...," she sobbed.

"I swear on my honour!" the lad insisted.

"I am not saying that you are indeed the culprit," Holmes interrupted. "At least for the present. The silhouette your mother saw could easily have belonged to Mr. Rossi, who has a similarly distinctive figure," Holmes turned his attention to the next object of his investigation.

The corpulent art historian was again tugging at his fingers in exasperation.

"I wonder what motive you have invented for me," he laughed unconvincingly.

"It might seem that you would be least interested in stealing a work of art that was destined to be in your custody, would it not?" Holmes chewed his pipe thoughtfully. "The Donatello was to be entirely at your disposal. It's very discovery secured you a place on the front pages of the newspapers and notoriety in curatorial circles which you had only to capitalise on with further study. If you had stolen the statue, you would never have been able to show it to anyone, and all these advantages would have been lost to you."

Rossi was relieved. "There you are."

"Of course, then there is vanity and a collector's obsession," Holmes developed the idea further. "The desire to own something so precious. You would be neither the first nor the last."

"That is utterly ridiculous," Salestro interjected.

"Perhaps, but not improbable," Holmes said, redirecting his attention, as the insurance agent seemed to be asking for it outright. "As for you, my dear fellow, you are indeed a prime candidate for the crime, as regards the expertise needed to pull it off. Handling the diamond cutter required to cut the glass? Only a professional would think of that. And I am well aware that the best insurance company employees are former criminal investigators... May I ask if you have ever worked for the police in the past?"

"Yes, I have, as you can readily ascertain," he admitted. "But that proves nothing."

"No indeed. Only that you were best equipped to do it. You were also the most familiar with the movements of the guards, and therefore knew how and when to avoid them. To procure Signore Montesutti's keys and slip into the gallery through the passage from the house, and arrange everything there to look like an intrusion from the outside, would have been a mere trifle for you. Nevertheless, we must not forget the master of the house..."

Alessandro Montesutti, who, collapsed in his chair, was listening to Holmes's explanation and discussion of possible motives with an expression of increasing torment, only raised his eyebrows.

"Insurance fraud?" he assured himself, as though knowing already what the detective was about to accuse him of.

"It is one of the most classic motives. If the warrior statue is not found, you shall collect a very large cheque, which you admitted to yourself," the detective nodded.

The head of the family raised no protest. The entire miserable group now sat before Holmes like a pack of whipped dogs, their Italian temperament seemingly having been replaced by French phlegmatism. Yet it was a mere pretence. All of them were undoubtedly suppressing a good deal of tension. The air was completely filled with the smoke and scent of the detective's pipe.

The carabiniere could make no sense of it all.

"I don't understand. Who do you blame then?" he asked Holmes, puzzled.

The detective made no reply, but asked the man at the drawing room door to fetch the night watchman, who had been waiting dutifully in the house ever since his interrogation.

"I will answer your question in a few moments," he announced to those present. "I need only ascertain one more thing."

By the time the guard arrived, the detective had prepared a chair for him and set up a small table behind it. He then seated the surprised man in the chair facing the audience, and on the table behind the watchman's back, he laid out a variety of items he had pulled from his pockets.

"Our only witness saw nothing, but he did hear something," Holmes pointed out. "If we can correctly identify the sound, it will give us a clue to the culprit."

I watched the faces of all, but I saw no fear of exposure in any of them.

"Let us first listen to the sound which occurred to the watchman as most fitting in comparison," said the detective, lifting from the table several twigs of varying thickness from the bushes in the garden. "The perpetrator could have brought a similar one in on his clothes and then stepped on it. Let's compare their sounds."

He broke each twig in turn behind the guard's back and waited to see if he would react to their snapping. However, the man shook his head in response to all the attempts.

"Just as I thought," Holmes acknowledged with satisfaction. "I had time to browse the garden, and found no sign of anyone trampling through it. This only further confirms my theory that no one actually came from there."

Next, he picked up a revolver and an encased knife.

"I am also taking into account the items the criminal might have had on his person at the time. Naturally, the thief may have brought something to defend himself with, and when the watchman approached, he might have readied his weapon before striking him," Holmes continued.

First he pulled back the hammer of the unloaded revolver, which clicked – with no reaction from the guard – and the same result was observed when he opened the snap on the knife case.

"What else, then, could be heard in the silence of the night?"

Holmes's sly grin suggested that he already knew. "The longer I thought about the sound, the clearer it became that it was probably a sound made unintentionally, by accident. After all, the culprit didn't want to give himself away."

"I beg you, do not keep us in suspense any longer!" Montesutti exclaimed.

The detective was not to be provoked, and continued to present the facts at his own pace.

"The floor had been freshly swept in the evening, and there was nothing on it but the shards of glass, but I have already ruled those out. Something on the perpetrator's body must have made the sound."

Holmes walked slowly round the watchman and stood behind his back again.

"Or it was the body itself!" he declared suddenly. At the words, he interlaced the fingers of both hands before our eyes, his arms outstretched and his palms rotated at ninety degrees.

There was a demonstrative crunch of knuckles.

The guard snapped to and cried out as he recognised the sound.

"It is a habit that the originator is no longer even aware of doing, or of the sound it makes," smiled the detective triumphantly as he, like the five suspects gathered about us, turned to the remaining one.

The perspiring Mr. Rossi's hands, which had been drumming away incessantly throughout Holmes's little performance, as they had been since the morning when we first met, emitted another incriminating "crunch." His mouth, conversely, could do no more than stammer.

"Looking at your hands, it is evident that you've suffered from this tic since a young age, and you cannot help it or control it. I assume that is why you dropped the piece of glass. People who crack their knuckles too often soon find them to be visibly swollen**," the detective confronted Rossi. "Before you struck the guard, you automatically cracked your knuckles without realising it."

Rossi was still striving to mumble something in his rising panic, but Holmes had no need for his confession.

"If you will allow me, I dare say I know why you stole the statue," he said. "The statuette, which you have so famously identified and which has allowed you to boast of a historic achievement, is not Donatello's work at all. I don't know whether you discovered your mistake at the outset or whether you only found it out later, but such an admission or revelation would turn the hero you now believe yourself to be into an amateur and a fraud. You couldn't afford to lose your reputation, which is why you needed the statue to disappear before it was moved to the museum, where it was to be subjected to a detailed examination."

Judging by the blueish hue of the historian's skin, Holmes was not far from the truth.

Ellena shrieked, Giacomo snorted derisively – perhaps relieved that the embarrassment that was to be shared with his uncle – and Montesutti rose menacingly before Rossi. On the whole, however, the family, whose professed harmony had taken a turn for the worse in the last few moments, seemed to have united against a common adversary.

The carabinieri officer and I proceeded forthwith to Rossi's room and began a thorough search, gradually revealing a set of black clothing, gloves and a glass cutter. I had the good fortune to be the finder of the last incriminating piece of evidence when I reached under the bed. It was only in the far corner that my fingertips finally fell upon the cool, bronze surface of the sought-after object, hastily wrapped in something or other.

Naturally, the statue never did make it to the museum and instead fell into oblivion again. The rest of our stay was – to Holmes's considerable displeasure – spent at a guest house in complete peace and seclusion.

Unfortunately, he received no reward.

* The god of travellers.

** The long-held belief that cartilage or bones make the crunching sound has been disproved. The sound is made by the space between the joints, filled with synovial fluid.

THE LAST VICTIM

OF JACK THE RIPPER

Our worst nightmare resurfaced only a few months after I had finally stopped waking in the middle of the night with my mind full of horrific images and jerking with fright at every unexpected murmur. The reign of the bestial killer known to the public as Jack the Ripper was over. And although I will most likely never be able to fully disclose the details of Holmes's involvement in the investigation of those heinous murders, nor the identity of their perpetrator, I was certain that the terrifying period culminating in the latter half of 1888 was over. I will only say that our shared secret of national importance* only strengthened the degree of mutual trust between myself and Sherlock Holmes. Even now, decades later, as I look back on this case, I can think of no other that has brought us closer together.

I assume that there is no one among my readers who is unfamiliar with the basic outlines of the entire mysterious case, so I do not intend to recount it in detail. The articles, the endless stream of new scholarly publications and novels inspired by the murders of easy women on the fringes of society seem unlikely to disappear from the shelves of newsagents and booksellers, even decades from now.

After solving the case, I asked myself whether the souls of the five unfortunate women – Mary Ann Nichols, Annie Chapman, Elizabeth Stride, Catherine Eddowes and Mary Jane Kelly – had ever found peace. Their murderer may have been identified thanks to Holmes, but he escaped classic secular justice by divine intervention. Frankly, I have been unable to give an honest reply to my question. Indeed, I myself was frustrated that in the eyes of the common folk, the shadow of Jack the Ripper had vanished into thin air without anyone having been officially charged, even though the newspapers had gradually dragged the names of several suspects through the mud without any direct evidence.

Those more knowledgeable may wonder why I mention five victims when there were allegedly many more... Indeed, there were several suspicious deaths in the broader vicinity at the time, but the threads leading directly from them to our killer were never proven beyond a shadow of a doubt or documented. Regardless of how many heinous acts Jack the Ripper committed, the law incriminated him for five deaths, and Holmes proved exactly the same number.

That is why it occurred to me, in the spring of 1889, whether the events I am now about to put on record for the first time may have been a portent from hell from those five women, making their displeasure known to us. For it was then that yet another body appeared.

The alleged sixth victim was found in the early hours of the morning in mid-March of 1889 in Pelham Street at Whitechapel, not far from the location we were better acquainted with than we would have liked following the previous year's investigation.

Before the panic could spread, Inspector Lestrade had a cab sent for us. It brought us to the scene on that Monday morning even before the arrival of Melville Macnaghten, Chief Constable of the Metropolitan Police Criminal Investigation Service, and Inspector Frederick Abberline, whom we had worked with on the Jack the Ripper case last year.

"How can this be, Holmes?" I asked as we travelled to the scene, shivering in part from the bitter morning cold, in part from the unevenness of the cobblestones, and in part from sheer anxiety. "We got the Ripper off the streets. There is no way he can still be killing!"

My friend, bundled in his blankets, kept his gaze fixed out of the window, but was looking at nothing in particular. Different scenes were unfolding before his eyes.

"And yet, we are presently on our way to see another body," he said quietly.

From the moment we had been awakened and dragged out of bed, a thought had been weighing on me that I couldn't shake. "What if we accused the wrong man back then?" I blurted.

Clearly we were both thinking the same thing.

"What can I say, Watson?" he sighed. "I am not so conceited as to think I can never be wrong. But I do have a natural confidence in my abilities, and however much I reassess my deduction, I don't believe I made a mistake. We must first obtain more data. I refuse to make hasty judgments and revise my conclusions so quickly."

He was right, of course, but even so, uneasiness had already been sown in my soul, and I, for one, did not arrive at the scene of the crime with a clear and unprejudiced mind, as would have been proper in view of the situation.

The carriage dropped us as close as possible to the site of the crime, as far as it could get, but even so the detective and I were obliged to walk down a stretch of narrow alley on our own. Our feet sank into a mixture of rubbish, mud and slops. Fortunately, none of the locals paid us any heed. Those who were already awake headed for a dark alcove by the door of a crumbling house, which was even now surrounded by a cordon of police.

Laying there like a discarded rag doll was the deceased, dark-haired young woman in a plain dress of forget-me-not blue, which the blood had soaked through in several patches to create dark patterns on the fabric. There was so much of the life-giving fluid around her that there could not have been much left in her body. It was consistent with the fact that those parts of the face and skin that weren't obscured or covered with a crust of dried, smeared blood were almost white.

We had not long since asked ourselves how any man could be capable of such a thing. Outwardly at least, we must have appeared dispassionate to the onlookers.

"Who discovered it?" Holmes promptly asked Lestrade, who was waiting for us.

The inspector beckoned to a constable pacing nearby, who told us how he had almost tripped over the body during his morning rounds, for it lay largely in the dark. Even on a clear day, the sun could not reach in among the cramped houses, let alone in the dim light of the cool dawn of coming spring.

I bent down to the poor woman to get a better look, brushing the matted hair from her forehead. Her eyes, almost as pale as her skin, showed a look of horror. Much of her face was smeared with blood from a long gash on her neck. Other abrasions and bruises were visible in several places on her neck and nape. Her attacker had apparently strangled her first and then slit her throat.

The blood, spurting from the artery as from a pump, had also splattered onto the wall of the alcove, down which it ran in rivulets. Even more of it oozed out from under her body from a second wound, the one that took us back in time by a quarter of a year – the wound that had prompted Lestrade to summon us, for the case appeared to be no ordinary murder, but the work of Jack the Ripper.

The dead woman's skirt was pulled up above her pelvis, which had been transformed into a mush of skin, flesh and tissue.

"Her womb has been excised," I announced to Holmes. "Very crudely and unsparingly, I would say. In any case, when the medical examiner arrives, I would suggest an autopsy, which will tell us more."

The words, addressed to the detective and the inspector, were overheard by the group of onlookers. One of the women issued an agonised yelp and almost fainted. Only a quick-witted constable saved her from collapsing into the muddy morass.

My friend walked up to the woman and patted her smudged cheeks lightly.

"Come on, wake up," he encouraged her. "Judging by your reaction, I believe you know who it is."

She groaned weakly, but recovered her senses and nodded apprehensively.

"She... her name was Monica... Monica Langley," she whispered fearfully.

"You knew her well?"

"She was... my roommate..."

"Do you live nearby?"

"Around the corner, just there," she pointed over her shoulder into what was perhaps an even narrower alcove.

"Interesting," Holmes mused, rubbing his chin. "Watson, can you determine when the murder took place?"

"I would say shortly before dawn, a few hours ago at the most," I deemed, judging by the onset of rigor mortis in the corpse.

"The same *modus operandi* as always," exclaimed an attentive Lestrade, eager to have something to report to his superiors. "Including the location chosen by the killer. A public place at a time when there is minimal danger of being disturbed."

"He was waiting for her as she returned home," the detective added. "I assume, given the nature of her occupation, that she spent her nights outdoors," he stated, focusing on the witness again. "Was this your usual turf?"

He spoke not from any distrust of the young and comparatively presentable young ladies living in this neighbourhood, who, after a thorough washing, might readily have graced the salons of even the wealthiest men, but simply from experience. Every one of Jack the Ripper's victims to date had been engaged in or associated with prostitution, which was why the killer had repeatedly, albeit not in all the cases, mutilated their bodies in a manner similar to what he had done to Monica Langley.

The woman, however, objected.

"I'm no whore," her cheeks flushed. "I'm a respectable woman!"

"May I know what your livelihood is?"

"I'm a waitress down at the pub."

Holmes grimaced doubtfully. "And Miss Langley?"

"I can't speak for her," she continued, frowning. "True, she wasn't home last night. But I never pried. She paid her dues, so what do I care what she did?"

"Might we visit your rooms?"

When she nodded, my friend turned to Lestrade.

"Please make a note of this woman's address in case your colleagues should wish to question her as well. The doctor and I will examine her quarters now and then see what happens. Should your men need me, I will be glad to be of service to them with my observations. Of course, knowing Inspector Abberline, he will want to follow his own clues and pursue the case on his own."

"As you please, Mr. Holmes," agreed the inspector. "I wanted you to see it for yourself. But you mustn't be surprised if Abberline and Macnaghten don't take advantage of your help this time. We may have been too quick in accepting your solution last time, whereas all the while the real Jack was waiting for us to drop our guard, so he could draw his knife again. This time, we won't be taken in by your fanciful deductions."

The detective did not deign to comment.

"Then I have only one piece of advice for you," he said. "Keep the newspaper hounds at bay for the present. You, too, will find it easier to work without a general uproar."

Lestrade took the advice, saying he was no novice, and graciously dismissed us.

We accompanied the woman, whom the inspector had jotted down as Shannon Hamblin, to her lodgings, situated roughly halfway down the block adjacent to Pelham Street. The rough-hewn door did very little to keep out the cold or rats, let alone uninvited visitors.

Then again, there was probably nothing to steal in a hovel like this.

Shannon and Monica lived on the first storey in a cramped room with only the most basic of amenities. A wash basin, a pitcher of water that was far from clean, a few garments hanging on lines, and a rickety chair. The two young women had slept on a single mattress on the floor, with a pillow of rags and a rough blanket. The room was heated with a small cast-iron stove, and differed but little from how most of the inhabitants of this poor neighbourhood lived in those days.

"Monica only moved in a few weeks ago," the lass told us. "She had stopped in for a drink at the King's Head, which is where I work, and asked if I knew of a place to stay. So I offered to let her stay with me for a while. I'm never in during the day, I come back late, and every penny counts, right?"

"Did she tell you anything about herself?"

"Like I said, we basically took turns," Shannon shook her head. "I slept here at night, she slept here in the mornings. We didn't have much opportunity to gossip. Not that she was the sort – a withdrawn, sullen, unhappy woman she was. Then again, aren't we all. Not much to be happy about around here."

"What do you think she did for a living?"

The woman mused. "Can't say. But I don't really think she was selling herself."

"What makes you say that?"

"She never – I mean, when she came home, and we did spend time together – she never smelled of any man. And believe me, I have a nose for those things," she confided. "She didn't have any diseases neither, like the crabs or such. I made sure."

"Quite so," Holmes reflected. "Where are her personal effects?"

Shannon pointed to a hanging dress. "Other than what she was wearing, she only brought her purse and a little silver locket of sorts. But I don't see them anywhere," she looked around.

"I'm certain there was nothing around her neck," I said, reviewing my examination in my mind.

"To date, the Ripper has never taken any trophies from his victims," the detective mused. "Of course, it's quite possible that the young woman simply dropped it and it's lying in the mud somewhere. Let us see if Abberline's people discover it."

The rickety boards creaked under my feet as I crossed the little room. Holmes cast me a reproachful glance, as though I were distracting him, but then paused. Something about the floor intrigued him.

He stooped where the planking was visibly ill-fitting and took hold of it. The plank lifted slightly without offering any resistance. A black purse lay in the hollow beneath.

"Here, here!" he exclaimed joyfully, lifting the purse from its hiding place and opening it.

Inside was a thick wad of notes.

"That's mine!" Hamblin held out her hand greedily for them.

Even I could tell she was lying.

The detective smiled. "What a remarkable coincidence. Just when we are searching for Miss Langley's purse, we find yours. Surely you know how much money there is here."

He hid the money behind his back and waited to see how the "respectable woman" would react.

"I've not counted it."

"Approximately, at least," he prompted her as she remained silent and gritted her teeth in annoyance.

"Very well then, I suppose it is Monica's," the woman said, resignedly. "I had no idea she was so flush with money. But surely you're not surprised that I tried my luck?" she attempted what was supposed to be an apology. "Won't do her any good anyway."

"As you have essentially proved to be helpful, I shall overlook this attempt at deception," said Holmes, slipping the purse under his coat. "The money will remain with me, and I will hand it over to the police. It may be a vital piece of evidence."

"Of what?" I asked, curiously.

"Do not get ahead of yourself, my dear Watson," he admonished me. "Miss Hamblin, one last question. Can you think of anyone who might know more about Monica after all?"

"Well, Frank O'Neill was quite taken with her, but surely he didn't kill her. He's just a clumsy oaf. He was at the pub when Monica first showed up and he never took his eyes off her. Just yesterday she complained that he kept following her about..."

"Excellent, ma'am," the detective rejoiced. "Doctor, would you be so kind, if you have any spare change on you, this does indeed deserve a reward," he requested.

I dropped the few coins I found in my pockets into Hamblin's hand, and we returned to the alley. From there, however, we started off in the opposite direction from which we had come, away from the dead woman's body and the growing swarm of police officers. From a distance, I could see Abberline, who had finally deigned to appear, barking orders and shooing away the intrusive curious onlookers and sensation hunters.

"Shouldn't we give them the money?" I inquired, hurrying after Holmes, who had dashed off.

"I should like to find Mr. O'Neill first," he replied. "I expect him to be at the King's Head. That place never closes, and its regulars seldom leave. If the police question Hamblin, she will surely tell them about the money."

His reluctance to help the Yard after what Lestrade had said was obvious.

"Would it not be better to get a handle on the suspects we put together in the previous Ripper investigation first?" I attempted to be rational.

"You heard them – they do not need my help, indeed they scorn it," he snorted. "They can manage on their own. What you suggest is clerical for someone as unimaginative as Abberline. I believe the key to the murderer lies in the dead woman's past."

"Murderer? We know who he is! Jack the Ripper!" I exclaimed.

The detective glanced warily about the street, teeming with a motley assembly of local laundry maids, servants, coachmen, labourers, tramps and more. All of them had yet another joyless day to survive. Their heads began turning after us.

"You must speak even louder," hissed Holmes. "There's a drunkard asleep on the sidewalk that didn't hear you."

I stumbled silently behind the fuming detective for a moment.

It was still relatively early in the morning, but life in the peripheral streets of the metropolis was already throbbing with a pulse of feverish activity. Some of the merchants were already displaying their wares, others were only just raising the shutters of their shops with a clatter. Even in the advancing light, however, the streets of Whitechapel were gloomy, dreary, broken down and reeking of a mixture of odours I had no desire to identify.

"Question marks, I should think, hover over both the killer and the motive. Does it not strike you as odd that Langley had so much money hidden under the floorboards? I can't help but wonder," the detective continued after a few minutes, when no one could hear us.

"She may have been saving up for a better life," I suggested.

"Those banknotes hardly look like something she saved up. I have counted the money, and it is far more than a poor soul like her could ever have earned. What's more, it is a pretty little round sum. No, it is either money she found or, far more likely, money she was given for something."

"So a prostitute after all?"

"For that amount, you could get the loveliest debutante, not some stodgy piece of work like Miss Langley," he argued.

Listening to Holmes, I had to admit he was right. It was all rather puzzling.

"With that kind of money, she could have afforded a much nicer place to live..."

"You speak my mind, Watson," he said gleefully, as if I had torn a blindfold from my eyes. "What does that imply? That the motive for her death may be the same as the reason she didn't spend her money. I believe she intended to pay it back. Whatever the reward may have been, Miss Langley seems to have changed her mind. Judging by the amount, it must have been something very substantial indeed."

"Which is why she went out every night," I pursued his line of reasoning. "Was she involved in the plotting of some crime or other? And then got scared?"

"It's not impossible," admitted the detective.

"Now we only need to find out how the Ripper fits in!" I exclaimed. "That O'Neill chap who's been stalking her must know where she's been going. He might have seen someone approach her!"

To this my friend made no further reply, for we were under the signboard at the King's Head.

***

Although less than an hour had passed since Shannon Hamblin had named the victim in front of the crowd of loafers, and we had hurried straight to the public house from her abode, the news had arrived before we did. The grapevine of the street had taken care of it.

The tavern guests were despondent. Instead of the usual boisterous imbibing, their only escape from the troubles of everyday life, there was now furtive whispering, if there was any talk at all. No one sang, no one played. The prospect that the serial killer had reappeared on the streets constricted everyone's throats. However, it was not enough to prevent Frank O'Neill, whom we recognised by the description, from swallowing several glasses of the cheapest liquor to quench his pain and anguish.

We sat down at his table, one on each side. There was plenty of room, for as soon as his cronies saw us approaching, they promptly rose from their seats. Holmes's face was no longer anonymous, nor was his service to law and order, and few of the local patrons had a clear conscience.

But none of the others interested us today.

"Mr. O'Neill, I understand you are going through a difficult time, but surely you too want Miss Langley's murderer to be caught. We need your help," Holmes addressed him.

The man in ragged and threadbare clothes barely noticed us and merely took a sip from his glass of clear liquid. Even at a distance I could smell the pungent odour of strong liquor.

"First off, I must ask what you were doing last night..." the detective continued.

"I don't want to interfere, gentlemen," the red-headed innkeeper approached us, clutching half a dozen foaming pints in one hand and a rag in the other. "But he won't tell you much. He's been drinking since yesterday. Been at it all night, and when the news about the girl came, he stopped talking altogether."

He automatically set two glasses in front of us and continued on his route, which began and ended at the tap. Along the way, he exchanged the empty mugs for full ones.

I leaned inconspicuously towards O'Neill and examined his boots, trousers and waistcoat. They apparently hadn't seen a washboard and soap in months, and there was plenty of dirt and mud on them, but no sign of blood. Nor were his hands, which could have loaded a coal wagon but recently how dirty they were, those of someone who had committed the butchery. Holmes made the same judgment.

"I hear you followed her round. Why?" Holmes inquired, shaking the man.

He sobbed. "No... I didn't want her to come to any harm... She was so... beautiful."

"It is essential that you tell us when you last saw her. Where did she go?"

O'Neill took another drink, but his lips had ceased to obey his mind. The spirit dribbled from his mouth down his chin, wetting his bedraggled beard. "She told me to bugger off, that she didn't ever want to lay eyes on me again," he droned on. "She said she was sick of all men," he poured his heart out, but slurring his words to such a degree that they were almost unintelligible.

"Where did she go?" the detective repeated, his voice raised in urgency.

"Somewhere in Knightsbridge. Almost every night, but I always lost her..." the drunkard managed to mutter before his head fell face down on the table-top.

I looked up. The neighbourhood in question is the polar opposite of Whitechapel. Many of London's richest people reside there, and if she hadn't been working for somebody there, the murdered woman must have looked as out of place as if Queen Victoria had stepped out of a carriage in the East End. If she was involved in anything that was going in in Knightsbridge, it was surely an important affair.

"Why, it's nearly a two hours' walk!" I exclaimed.

"It is a testimony to Miss Langley's determination that she made the journey every night. We must go at once," decided Holmes.

We paid for the ale, which we hadn't even touched, and whistled for a cab to take us away from the hovel. I confess I was relieved when we pulled into the wider streets of the city centre with their tidy cobblestones and bright facades.

"We should focus on all the major events going on in Knightsbridge, like art or jewellery exhibitions. She might also have been spying on a jewellery store, or checking on the police officers' rounds, where they are at what time," I suggested.

Holmes listened to me with an air of delight regarding my plan, but not for long.

"Unless the deed has already been done," he demolished my theory.

As we were already passing through the streets of Knightsbridge, he stopped the cab and we set off on foot.

We were heading for the local police station, but in the end were spared the visit, for we met one of the senior officers of the constabulary, with whom we had collaborated on a case in the past and who held my friend in high esteem. We discussed the matter with him from all aspects, but to no avail.

"We've not dealt with any major robberies lately. And there will be no guarded exhibitions in the coming days or weeks," mused the policeman.

I was just resigning myself to the idea that we would have to go round all the jewellery shops in person – and there were quite a few in this neighbourhood – to inquire about any forthcoming major deliveries of wares, when Holmes asked the officer a crucial question.

"By the way, Officer, have you ever heard the name Monica Langley?"

"Langley... Langley...," the officer mused. "Wait, you mean the tramp?"

"That would be the one," the detective said. "Have you met her?"

"Not in person, I only know her name from reports. A completely intoxicated woman had been disturbing the peace for several nights in succession. Lord Katleman even filed a complaint about a person by that name. My men went to fetch her from outside his house, and explained to her emphatically that she had no business in our neighbourhood. She was talking nonsense, but our men shut her foul mouth," he laughed cynically.

I didn't dare to imagine what such a reprimand might have looked like, and glanced instead at my watch. By this time, the doctor was surely taking the body in for an autopsy. At least half of the bruises on the body would not have been perpetrated by the killer.

Holmes's warmth likewise faded at those words, and we parted with the policeman coldly. I believe he failed to realise that he had said something we could not approve of, and he merely saluted politely and strode off to his duties.

"Lord Katleman is one of the wealthiest residents of Knightsbridge," mused the detective. "So we know who she had set her sights on."

"Shall we pay him a visit?"

"Naturally," he replied. "Our investigation has just taken an unexpected turn!"

"Whatever do you mean?"

"Until now, we have assumed she came here to observe someone or something. That requires stealth. But she was disturbing the peace of the night and, on the contrary, calling attention to herself quite volubly. Another mystery that doesn't fit our theories at all. Perhaps we can find out from His Lordship, why she behaved as she did."

The elderly Lord Katleman resided in a magnificent Victorian house near Hyde Park. After ringing the bell, a rather stuffy butler answered the door, annoyed that we had come at a rather inconvenient time, as the gentleman was about to take his luncheon.

"We shan't be but a minute. We only want to know why you summoned the police," Holmes told him.

"I don't believe I understand you," said the man sternly.

"According to the report, Lord Katleman summoned the police to deal with a certain Monica Langley, who was making a nuisance of herself in front of your house," the detective reiterated, repeating what he knew from the policeman.

"I can assure you that in the twenty years I have served and lived in this house there has been no such scandal or any other," scowled the butler still more, and was about to slam the door, when a young, industrious maid appeared behind his back, having overheard our conversation.

"I expect the gentlemen would like to see Lord Katleman's son. Monica used to be in his service," she said.

"That may be," admitted the detective.

"The young gentleman and his family live elsewhere. You must go several streets over," the butler referred us to another address.

"I was not aware that young Lord Katleman also owned a house in this neighbourhood," I said in surprise.

"He only recently received it from his father, when his wife finally came with child and bore him an heir," escaped the maid's mouth. "The old man wanted peace and quiet, but he also wanted to keep them nearby. He adores the little one. Why, he was miserable before for fear that the family lineage would die out on the spear side! He was even considering going so far as to punish and disinherit the young master."

"That's quite enough, miss," the butler shushed her quickly. "You're not at market here, nor in the social column of some tabloid rag. Such indiscretion is strictly out of the question! And you, gentlemen, be on your way!"

Hence we found ourselves back on the street, and proceeded to move on to the next address.

"I am beginning to feel that things are getting increasingly convoluted, and that we are getting somewhat distracted from the murder investigation. We will hardly find the Ripper here, after all," I complained, as fatigue and frustration crept over me.

In spite of the gravity of the situation, Holmes laughed, rather inappropriately to my taste.

"Indeed. Whereas I believe this will be our final visit, which will provide us with some rather significant answers!" he predicted. I trusted he was not mistaken.

Unfortunately, it wasn't all that simple.

***

"Everett Katleman. What can I do for you, gentlemen?" the tall, blond aristocrat with angular features and prominent cheekbones said, introducing himself.

"We are here on behalf of one Monica Langley," announced Holmes in the anteroom of the man's house, which was indeed no more than a fifteen minutes' walk from his father's residence.

Katleman did not bat an eyelid.

"I'm afraid I am not acquainted with any such person," he said.

The detective cleared his throat dryly, without letting his bemusement show.

"Rather odd, considering you summoned the police to deal with a person of that very name but a few days ago," he remarked. "All the more so as she is your former housemaid."

The lord's skin, already rather pale, seemed to become even paler, but he continued to maintain an admirable poker face.

"Ah, that one," he exclaimed, "remembering" suddenly. "Many servants have come and gone through my house, and I cannot possibly remember them all. But it is true that this young woman made some trouble."

"What sort of trouble?"

Katleman noticed that the maid who had come to open the door had remained in the hall with us, her ears very much perked.

"Come in, gentlemen, I do not care to discuss this matter in the doorway," he beckoned. "And you, Linette, fetch us some tea. Then you can set the table for lunch."

We were ushered into the drawing room where a slight woman sat in a chair by a tall window. She was cradling an infant in her arms – a boy, judging by the blue colour of his swaddling clothes, who could not have been more than a few weeks old. She was softly humming a melodious lullaby and stroking his dark, thick hair affectionately.

"My wife, Gladys," the lord introduced her.

Lady Katleman glanced at us, putting a forefinger to her lips as a sign that we should not wake the child. She took him gently and carried him off to a quieter part of the house.

"He is the apple of our eye, a darling child," the proud father beamed, taking a seat on the divan. As we settled in, I noticed that he had a slight limp.

Before the maid brought in the teapot and three cups, we exchanged a few pleasantries, as two war veterans, about where we had served and what injuries we had sustained, while the detective perused the family portraits on the wall.

Then, without further ado, he began speaking. I had the sense that he didn't care to give His Lordship too much time to prepare his answers.

"Let us return to Miss Langley," he requested. "You mentioned certain difficulties."

"I do not wish to smear the affair, as I wouldn't like to cause her any more trouble," Katleman waved his hand. "Her work ethic was far from exemplary, and we did not part on good terms. She is a temperamental young woman, and she used to come here to vent her anger. Nothing to occupy the mind of a private investigator."

"We are here because she was murdered. In a very brutal fashion, I might add," said Holmes. "You must admit that this is worthy of my attention."

The nobleman, pouring himself some tea, started and spilled it over his trousers and part of the table. He seemed genuinely surprised by the information, but my friend was a far better reader of human reactions with a great deal more experience. However, he did not let on whether he perceived it as a guise or genuine surprise.

"I am sorry to hear that, naturally," Katleman said. "But I had nothing to do with it."

The detective drew out his handkerchief and spread it over the spilled tea before it soaked into his trousers or into the pile of letters laying on the edge of the table under a paperweight.

"Leave that alone, Linette will take care of it," the lord rang the bell to summon the maid.

Holmes had not yet finished. He reached into his coat and took out the purse stuffed with banknotes.

"Do you know where she could have obtained so much money?" he asked, showing it to our host.

"Indeed I do not," Katleman retorted brusquely. "Why are you asking me about all this, anyway?"

"Because you are the only person of her acquaintance who could dispose of such a sum."

His Lordship looked offended. "Acquaintance? I beg you, I haven't seen that woman for three quarters of a year! We were not acquainted, as you put it. I did not wish her any harm, but after how she behaved, I am sincerely relieved that my family will finally find peace."

"Very well, then. I can think of no further questions. For the present," added Holmes meaningfully.

We were shown out, but the detective paused again on the threshold.

"I understand that it must be unpleasant for someone in your position to be associated with a murder, let alone of a girl so far beneath you on the social ladder, but I must warn you that the circumstances of her death are of interest to those in the highest places. You may soon receive a visit from my colleagues at the Metropolitan Police. I am certain they will do their utmost not to cause a scandal."

Everett Katleman took note of Holmes's words, and undoubtedly hoped that he would never see us again.

We crossed the busy street to the outskirts of Hyde Park, where a refreshment stand stood in the shade of the trees.

"Would you care for a sandwich, Watson?" the detective asked.

I had little appetite after the morning's exploits and examination of the corpse, but could not deny that my stomach had started growling.

"Excellent," he acknowledged. "I suggest you enjoy it here on the bench. In the meantime, I would like to ascertain something. We shall meet again, say at four o'clock, outside the city morgue. Do you agree?"

I had no reason to object. "But you insist that I have my lunch right here?"

"If you would indulge me. You see, from here you have an ideal vantage point to observe the entrance to Katleman's residence. I want to test whether my words truly left him as indifferent as he pretended to be, or whether they provoked him into action."

I recognised the ruse and selected a roast beef and pickle sandwich on brown bread from the stand. I'd been assigned to considerably less appealing stations than sitting on a sunny bench in a city park on a chilly late morning, so I was quite content.

Holmes departed, and I chose a bench for lunch from which I had a clear view of the street while myself remaining inconspicuous. For half an hour, nothing at all happened and I was beginning to think the detective's experiment had failed – either because Katleman indeed had naught to do with Langley and her death, or because he had excellent nerves.

Then suddenly, the door opened and His Lordship stepped out.

He was wearing only a light coat, suggesting he didn't intend to venture far. My first thought was that he was going to visit his father, but it was not so. He looked around stealthily and walked briskly down the street. At Hyde Park Corner, however, he stepped into an intersection and headed straight for the park, where I nearly lost him, but his tall figure in a top hat, characterised by a swaying gait, soon reappeared in one of the tree-lined lanes heading into the deeper reaches of the park. Further away from the crowd, the young lord slowed down; his leg injury would likely have prevented him from keeping up so brisk a pace for long. Consequently, I had no trouble following him to the deserted Serpentine.

There he looked around again before pulling something from his pocket and hurling it into the water.

We had to retrieve it!

I stared intently at the spot where the object had sunk, and once Katleman was gone I marked it with branches carefully positioned on the bank. Then I set off to fetch a gang of street urchins, who were kicking a ball around on the lawn not far off.

"I know it's rather chilly, but if you can fish something out of the lake, you will earn a handsome reward," I coaxed them, encouraging them by holding up a shiny sovereign.

They did not require much persuading, and I led them back to the body of water that divides Hyde Park in two and showed them where to search.

"Is this some sort of challenge? You couldn't have dropped anything that far from the shore," said one of the cocky, imp-eyed boys with his arms folded defiantly across his chest. When I doubled the promised reward, the boys obediently threw off their overcoats and jumped into the water in naught but their undergarments.

I felt somewhat ashamed, but from a purely medical perspective I decided that such bracing would do them no harm. After all, it was March already, and not the dead of winter.

After a few minutes of diving, the chilled boys with chattering teeth brought me what I was looking for and handed it over in exchange for the money. In my wet palm glistened a silver locket, the very one described as belonging to Miss Langley.

It could only mean that Lord Katleman was Jack the Ripper.

***

I could hardly wait until four o'clock, when Holmes and I were to meet outside the morgue. I thought he'd come out from inside, assuming he would have gone in to hear the results of the autopsy from the medical examiner, but to my surprise, he was only just heading in.

"Let us go together, Watson. Your opinion is important to me," he called to from the cab that had just delivered him to our destination.

I was eager to inform him at the earliest opportunity of my discovery, which *de facto* incriminated Katleman, but before he could pay the coachman and turn his attention to me, Lestrade emerged from the morgue.

"What are you gentlemen doing here?" he inquired haughtily. "A case, perhaps?" he added sardonically.

"I am rather interested in what conclusions your doctor has drawn in the Langley case," the detective replied in greeting.

"I'm afraid I can't tell you that," the inspector dismissed him with a self-important air. "At Chief Constable Macnaghten's request, we will tie up the case ourselves. This time, to a victorious end, may I point out. Abberline is sure of it. We've pinched that Polish Jew before, and he has no alibi this time. There will be no escaping the noose."

He was referring to Aaron Kosminski, one of the prime suspects during the original search for the Ripper, along with Thomas Cutbush, an addled medic suffering from syphilis, and Charles Lechmere, a butcher. All the suspects at the time shared a deep-rooted hatred of women and severe psychological disorders, but there was no irrefutable evidence against any of them, and Holmes finally pointed the finger at someone else entirely.

"I can only advise you not to be too hasty," Holmes warned him.

"Like you, isn't that right? Don't worry, we're in no danger of that. We are professionals."

"Quite so. I have no need to see the results of the autopsy anyway. I already know what they contain."

With this statement, the detective utterly disarmed the inspector.

"Oh? Let's hear it then," Lestrade sneered.

"At the crime scene, Dr. Watson here already noted that Monica Langley had been killed somewhat less expertly than Jack the Ripper's previous victims. Whereas before, the killer had worked with obvious knowledge of anatomy and precision, this time he was driven by rage. Several older bruises from a brutal cudgel beating were also found on her body. And I suspect it is not without interest that the lady had recently given birth."

The inspector opened the report he was carrying under his arm and glared at my friend.

"How can you possibly know this? I only got the report myself a few minutes ago!"

"I am a professional," the detective replied jovially and tipped his hat in farewell.

We left Lestrade standing dumbstruck on the pavement outside the morgue, taking advantage of the fact that the cab Holmes had taken had not yet departed. We leapt in, and the detective gave the address from which I had just arrived.

"How did you know she was pregnant?"

"Patience, my friend! We shall be on the spot in a moment, and I will lay it all out for you there."

"So you already know it was Katleman?"

"I should say it's practically a certainty. How did you fare? Was your mission a success?"

I described to him all that had occurred near the little lake in the park, and handed him the locket.

"Excellent, Watson, excellent indeed!" he complimented me. "As always, you have proved yourself most helpful."

"Not at all. It was your genius that led you to realise that Katleman was the Ripper," I returned the compliment. "We've finally got him."

Holmes was astonished. "The Ripper? Who ever said he was the Ripper?"

"Why, you just said so!"

"My dear Doctor. Your and Lestrade's obsession with the Ripper prevents you from seeing things in a broader context," he complained. "Let us go over the facts together. All of Jack the Ripper's proven victims were fallen women, correct? There can be no argument about that. And what do we know about Miss Langley?"

"That she wasn't a prostitute, but an ordinary housemaid who, conversely, kept men at bay," I admitted.

"Besides, the Ripper demonstrated countless times that he attacks only one type of woman, and kills them with a very precise knowledge of the anatomy of the human body," he reminded me. "We've also overlooked the fact that in the past, he has always killed at the end of the month and before the weekend. In this case, none of the characteristic concomitant phenomena typical of the Ripper's actions have been satisfied, no matter what the deluded Lestrade says."

"Whatever do you mean?"

"I mean that it was a brutal, heinous murder, but in no way connected with Jack. Once I accepted that thesis, it allowed me to look at the case with fresh eyes."

"And what do you see?"

"A handmaid who accidentally falls pregnant and confides this to the couple she serves, who are striving in vain for a child of their own. A couple that cannot have children and face the threat of disinheritance by the head of the family, who demands the continuation of the family lineage. So they offer to provide a life of prosperity for her child, and pay her a hefty indemnity in exchange. They will take care of her somewhere in seclusion until she gives birth. Meanwhile, the lady feigns her own pregnancy. When the handmaid hands over the newborn child as agreed, they send her away. She is not allowed to tell a soul about it if she wishes to avoid trouble herself. But then the girl's maternal instinct is aroused and she wants her baby back. She returns repeatedly to her former employer's house, offering to return all the money, of which she hasn't spent a penny. She pleads, for better or worse, and starts drinking out of sheer grief. In desperation, she even attempts to break into their house, so they summon the police. But the husband foresees that the trouble may escalate, and decides to get rid of her once and for all."

"Good God!" I gasped. Of course, it all made sense.

"You saw both the corpse, and the child Lady Gladys was cradling," Holmes recalled. "The Katlemans are fair-haired, almost of the Anglo-Saxon type, as are all the members of their family, as we could see in the portraits on the walls of the house. The child had dark hair, like Langley's. Incidentally, based on other anthropological features, she does not fit in with their clan at all."

"Still, that is no proof!" I realised.

"Indeed it is not. I confess that I procured the proof by employing two contrivances," he revealed.

"You provoked Katleman into getting rid of the evidence."

"I had hoped he still had the locket. Where else would it be? Perhaps, somewhat irrationally, he wanted his son to have something that belonged to his real mother."

"And the other ruse?"

"I originally worked with the assumption that Katleman might be the child's father and Langley may have been his mistress. However, I noticed a letter atop of a stack of papers on the table in the drawing room, with an address from a women's doctor. Unfortunately, I had to compromise medical confidentiality in order to discover the murderer, and while you were keeping watch in Hyde Park, I broke into his surgery. In the Katleman file, I learned that Lord Katleman's war injuries had taken a toll on his reproductive abilities, nor had nature been kind to Lady Gladys in this regard. It is biologically impossible for them to have a child. They cannot justify its existence."

"Why didn't they simply adopt a child? The orphanages are full of them!"

"I expect old Lord Katleman would hardly approve of such a solution. He insisted on the bloodline."

The blood of the Katleman dynasty was to be preserved before the outside world by shedding the blood of the poor handmaid. "It is monstrous," I said, shuddering with disgust.

"The worst of it is that I have no doubt the Katlemans truly and sincerely love the child. It was the one thing they had not to pretend when they received us."

"What will happen to the little one now? Will he be sent to an orphanage?"

"I dare not guess," Holmes rubbed his tired eyes and glanced out of the cab to see if we were nearing Knightsbridge. "Let us get it over with!"

At the Katlemans' residence, the familiar housemaid opened the door for us.

"You are Linette, are you not?" Holmes addressed her sharply. "Tell me, quickly, if you do not wish to be held an accomplice, where was His Lordship last night?"

"At h-h-home," she cried, startled.

"You are lying!"

"I s-swear, I brought him up valerian d-drops to help him sleep," she stammered.

He scowled at her sternly and entered without permission. His behaviour was almost menacing.

"But the lady left sometime after midnight, I heard her dressing," the maid managed to gasp.

My pupils dilated. So Katleman wasn't the murderer – it was his wife? That was why it took him almost an hour to step out and get rid of the evidence. He learned of his wife's crime after our visit, and only then did he confront her. He also took from her the locket she had torn from Monica's neck.

The master of the house appeared in the stairwell leading up from the hall. "I do believe I'd made myself clear!" he snapped angrily. "Stop harassing us!"

"And I believe I made myself clear that your title would not stop the investigation of a murder," Holmes retorted. He then displayed the silver locket, fished out from the bottom of the Serpentine.

"Please stop shouting in here," said Lady Gladys, emerging from the drawing room bearing the swaddled child.

"Gladys, they know everything," sobbed the aristocrat.

"Let me put Cecil to bed, and then we can talk it over," the lady said, giving us with a look so replete with affection that we could not refuse her.

We did not believe she would deny the facts or attempt an escape, and followed Katleman into the sitting room. In the meantime, Holmes sent the housemaid Linette to the police station to summon a patrol.

Katleman steeled himself and poured out several glasses brandy to calm everyone down. As it was already late in the afternoon, we gladly accepted.

"What now?" he asked with a dignified jut of his chin.

"We shall have to arrest you," said the detective. "Both of you."

"And the boy?"

"The authorities will take care of him. His mother is dead and the father is unknown."

From behind our backs came a woman's calm voice, accompanied by the characteristic click of a revolver hammer, which Lord Katleman, like any proper, albeit retired, soldier, surely had somewhere in the house. "I will never give him up!" the lady announced.

Her forefinger trembled on the trigger of the heavy weapon, which she had to hold with both hands.

"Darling, we must be reasonable," Katleman stepped towards his wife, anxious to comfort her and take the weapon away.

Unfortunately, instead of reason, Lady Gladys was overwhelmed by emotion and horror at the thought of losing her cherished child. Her mind, addled by anguish, assessed her husband's approach as an imminent threat. She turned her extended arms, grasping the Enfield army revolver, away from us and towards Katleman, and fired blindly.

There was a report, the lady staggered, and a bloodstain began to seep through the Lord's vestment in the middle of his chest, right over the heart. He never even flinched and slumped to the ground as if his legs had been pulled from under him.

There were enough bullets left in the cylinder for Lady Katleman to eliminate any obstacles and witnesses to her husband's killing at once – Holmes and myself. My friend took a step forward, shielding me from possible gunfire with his body. But his heroic gesture was unnecessary. The lady trembled and continued to clutch her weapon, but she was not going to shoot – at least not at anyone else.

Staring at her hands as if in disbelief at what she had just done, she sank to her knees beside her husband's prostrate body, her eyes moist with tears. She scooped a drop of blood from his waistcoat onto her fingertips and rubbed it between her thumb and index finger.

"It's over," she gasped.

Then she glanced at us, agitated.

"Promise me he will have a good life," she said, and before we realised what she was doing, it was too late.

Gladys Katleman took the revolver in both hands again, placed the barrel under her chin, and pulled the trigger.

***

Whenever I drive through Knightsbridge or past Hyde Park, I remember. We did what we thought was right. When Linette returned with the police patrol, we gave them only as much information about the two dead bodies as we deemed necessary.

It was beyond us to plunge into a life of misery and misfortune a child merely several weeks old, who had lost his mother through no fault of his own, and whose new parents who had literally stepped over dead bodies to have him.

We described Lord and Lady Katleman's involvement in the death of Monica Langley as the tragic culmination of a love affair and suicide to avert a scandal. Although Abberline and his men strove on for some time to link the case to Jack the Ripper, the inspector himself eventually admitted that the theory was unfeasible, and confirmed Holmes's non-public conclusions of the previous year. He made an unofficial apology to my friend.

Little Cecil was taken in by his only living relative, Grandfather Katleman, in good faith.

It had been a very long day for Holmes and I, and we were glad it was over.

"I gather that it was not Katleman who took the locket from Monica, but rather his wife, for the same reason that you have ascribed to him. Lady Katleman took a great risk in going to Whitechapel alone at night, but what I don't understand is whether she mutilated Monica Langley's body to distract attention. Was she hoping we would pursue the ghost of Jack the Ripper?" I mused aloud on the way home.

Holmes shook his head sadly.

"I don't believe the lady made any such cold-blooded plans; it was all the act of a woman driven mad," he shrugged. "Langley wanted to take from her that without which her life was worthless. She envied her not just that one particular child, but the ability to mother a child as such. It wasn't enough for her to kill the poor girl as a human being, she hated her for doing what she couldn't – giving birth to another life. That is why, most likely in an act of affectation, she mutilated her in the uterine region. She cut out her womb and then disposed of it somewhere."

Desperate women do desperate things.

"At least the Ripper never actually returned," I sighed.

"Only in our distraught imaginations," Holmes nodded. "We can both rest easy that we identified the real Jack the Ripper long ago, and that there was no mistake. The perpetration of evil has been ingrained in the nature of mankind since the days of Cain and Abel, so we shall certainly continue to encounter murders, even very heinous ones, but the perpetrators will be different. And I will never stop searching for them," he added firmly.

Back in Baker Street, we had another nightcap and sat by the hearth for some time.

That night, we and the residents of Whitechapel, faced by countless challenges every day of their lives – poverty, disease, inadequate sanitation, malnutrition and more – were able to forget at least one worry and sleep soundly again. But surely no one in Monica Langley's circle would ever have dreamt that the heir to one of our nation's oldest and wealthiest noble families, who now sits in the House of Lords and co-determines their fate, has not a drop blue blood in his veins, but instead the blood of one of their own – a murdered former housemaid and an unknown tramp.

The kind reader will therefore pardon me for altering the family's real name for the purposes of this story. I do not wish to be responsible for another political scandal.

* The Doctor's seemingly innocent remark suggests an existing theory that Prince Albert Victor, son of the then heir to the throne and later King Edward VII, was somehow involved in the murders.

Milton Keynes UK
Ingram Content Group UK Ltd.
UKHW020334081124
450874UK00010B/502